HER SECRET SELF

"Cliff Wright sure is impressive looking," Joanne whispered.

"Hmm, do I detect some interest here?" Lynn asked hopefully. "It's about time you got Rob off your mind."

"I haven't given up on Rob," Joanne explained. "I was just wondering what he would do if he saw me hanging out with Cliff."

"So why don't you forget Rob and go out with Cliff?"

"I'll never stop loving Rob," Joanne insisted. "Cliff's just a friend."

"I think you're making a mistake, Joanne. Rob's getting tighter with Christina every day."

"You're wrong. It won't last once Rob gets reminded of the good times we had."

"Well, don't come to me for any ideas," Lynn responded. "You're on your own now, kid."

Her Secret Self

Rhondi Vilott

BANTAM BOOKS
TORONTO • NEW YORK • LONDON • SYDNEY

RL 5, IL age 11 and up

HER SECRET SELF

A Bantam Book / November 1982

ISBN 0-553-22543-X

Published simultaneously in the United States and Canada

*Bantam Books are published by Bantam Books, Inc. Its trademark,
consisting of the words "Bantam Books" and the portrayal of a
rooster, is Registered in U.S. Patent and Trademark Office and in
other countries. Marca Registrada. Bantam Books, Inc., 666 Fifth
Avenue, New York, New York 10103.*

PRINTED IN THE UNITED STATES OF AMERICA

O   0 9 8 7 6 5 4 3 2

Her Secret Self

Chapter One

Joanne Palmer gazed longingly at the dark-haired boy two rows over and three seats up, but he continued to ignore her. Rob McAllister, her ex-boyfriend.

Joanne sighed. It was bad enough to have to return to another boring semester at Fremont High—her last—but to be stuck in study hall with Rob was sheer torture. *Study hall . . . what a joke!* There was no way she could even attempt to study with Rob in the same room. Yet that's exactly what her parents expected her to do.

Miss Thornton, the study hall teacher, sat at the front of the room, her nose in a book, seemingly oblivious to the rising decibel level in the room. She stretched one blue-veined hand in front of her, gripping a wooden ruler that she relinquished only to turn a page.

A kick at the back of her chair interrupted Joanne's thoughts. She turned around to meet her friend Lynn Willis's inquiring glance. "Rob say anything yet?" Lynn whispered.

Joanne shook her head, her dark hair falling in her eyes for the umpteenth time that day. "He's been ignoring me all week. In English this morning he even moved his seat so he didn't have to sit near me. Lynn, what am I going to do?"

Her friend gave her a "buck-up" pat. "We'll think of something."

"It'd better be quick. He's breaking my heart."

Miss Thornton's forehead furrowed, and her hand twitched on the ruler as the noise level continued to rise.

Suddenly the sharp buzz of the interoffice phone broke through the noise. The study hall teacher looked up, and her long nose twitched as she snatched up the phone before it could buzz again.

Joanne threw another longing glance in Rob's direction. He was the only boy she wanted—she was convinced of that—but he didn't want her anymore. Sighing, she slouched down in her chair, remembering the last time he had kissed her and how warm, secure, and loved it had made her feel. To Joanne that kiss had signaled the beginning of an even deeper, more meaningful relationship. Instead, Rob had broken up with her shortly afterward. Even so, Joanne hadn't given up hope that she might win him back. A boy who kissed her like that had to truly love her.

Miss Thornton put down the phone and startled Joanne out of her daydream. "Miss Palmer! Come up here, please."

"Uh-oh, Joanne," Lynn said.

Joanne dropped her book and bolted upright in her chair. "Me?"

Miss Thornton nodded briskly, her eyes already wandering back to the book she held in her hand. She looked up again when Joanne reached her desk. "Please report to the counseling office," she told her.

"Yes, Miss Thornton," Joanne answered, wondering what they wanted this time.

Joanne went back to her seat, ignoring Lynn's expression of concern as she stooped to retrieve her books. After she stood up, she once again brushed her hair out of her eyes, vowing it would be the last time she'd "do" Brooke Shields. She and Lynn often pretended to be famous people, dressing and acting like them for a day. Doing Brooke had been Lynn's idea, but Joanne found herself wondering how Brooke ever saw where she was going.

As she walked toward the door, Joanne

glanced back at Lynn. "Good luck," Lynn said in a whisper.

A chunky, blond boy tapped Joanne's elbow on her way out. "Want to come to my house tomorrow night? A bunch of us are going to listen to records."

"Sounds neat, Frank. I'll call and let you know." For the last time, she glanced over at Rob, who was bent over a book, ignoring her completely.

On the way to the counseling office, Joanne pulled a tissue out of her pocket and wiped some of the excess "Brooke" makeup off her eyes, being careful not to smudge her mascara. It was bad enough, she thought, to have to deal with Rob's ignoring her—but a call to the office! Not that it was totally unexpected. Joanne had had a slightly less than perfect academic career, and by now she couldn't remember the number of times she'd been called down to discuss her "problem."

As she made her way down the hall, balancing her stack of textbooks first in the crook of one arm, then in the other, she tried to pinpoint what the problem could be. Surely there were no troubles in advanced home ec., the only course in which she had maintained a B average. And PE was a snap—all she had to do to pass was show up. She thought she was keeping her head above water in business math, too. So it had to be bad news in one of the big ones—English or history. She sighed again, flicking away another strand of hair. *I'll bet these things never happen to Brooke,* she thought. *Only to me.*

Still balancing her books, Joanne stuffed the tissue back into her jeans pocket as she reached the administrative offices. She shouldered open the door to the counseling office and paused at the side of the secretary's counter. Mrs. Beal didn't even look up as she said, "Joanne, Ms. Kovelstein is waiting for you. It's the last office."

She must have seen me coming, Joanne thought. She started to nod a thank you but ended up mumbling one instead. Kovelstein, she had heard, was a new counselor, a midyear replacement. Joanne forced a smile, trying her best to look optimistically at the situation. Maybe she could get a fresh start with a new counselor!

The smile vanished, however, as she pushed open the door, books swaying in her arms, and saw that Ms. Kovelstein wasn't alone. Sitting in the chair next to the counselor's desk was Joanne's mother.

"Hi, Mom," Joanne said cautiously. Whatever it was, she must have really done it this time! They called her mother in only on the big ones.

"Why, Joanne. Come in," Ms. Kovelstein said pleasantly.

5

Joanne's mother looked at her silently. She was not smiling.

"Ms. Kovelstein," Joanne said, determined to be cheerful, "it's nice to have somebody modern around. Does Ms. stand for Miss or Mrs.?"

"We'll discuss me later," the woman behind the desk said briskly. "Let's concentrate on *you* first."

Ms. Kovelstein was about as old as Joanne's mother. She had obviously just moved in, because the office was cluttered with unpacked boxes; there was even a pile of tennis equipment on the floor in one corner. Joanne watched nervously as the counselor leafed through the folder in front of her. *My dossier*, thought Joanne.

The counselor's expression softened as she faced the pretty girl. "As you know, Joanne, I'm new here at Fremont. When problems come up, I intend to follow the customary procedure of contacting and working with the student first and calling in the parents only if necessary. However"—she paused, her fingernails tapping the file—"here I have had to make an exception."

"That's all right. Mom's pretty understanding. Right, Mom?" But Joanne felt a chill down the back of her neck. From the look on her mother's face, she had an awful suspicion her mother wasn't going to be so understanding this time.

"I would say your mother is a paragon of

patience." Ms. Kovelstein smiled ruefully. "Your senior-class status is shaky, as you know. Every year there have been certain classes you haven't passed and have had to make up. Your summer grades were acceptable—barely—but there's a problem with the semester of American history you just repeated."

"A problem?"

"You failed it. Again."

"Oh, Joanne," said her mother, speaking for the first time. "Is it possible?"

"Well—" Joanne looked from parent to counselor. It didn't seem fair. It must have been that test she took before Christmas vacation that had done her in, she thought. It was the day after Rob told her he was breaking up with her. She was sure she'd been passing the course up to that point. Slumped in the chair, she added, "Yeah, it's possible. But all Mr. Sheldon ever cared about was the Civil War. Details and details—dates and names and places. How could anyone have memorized them all? I mean, isn't the important thing that the North won?"

Ms. Kovelstein cleared her throat. "It would have been nice if your final exam had indicated that fact."

"It didn't?" She stared in horror at Ms. Kovelstein's desk.

Mrs. Palmer was startled. "Joanne, how could you?"

"I'm afraid that's only one of the many questions you answered incorrectly."

"That can't be true," Joanne said and sighed. "Then again, maybe it is true." She was going to have to talk with Lynn about her system for taking multiple-choice exams. Something obviously had gone wrong in a major way.

Mrs. Palmer shifted in her chair, a sign that she was getting ready to do battle. Joanne relaxed slightly. Her mother could be stern, but she was always on Joanne's side. Well, usually.

"What does that mean?" her mother asked, concerned.

Ms. Kovelstein tilted her head to one side as she closed the folder. "It means Joanne won't be able to double up with her civics and economics classes this semester the way we had hoped. She still has to get a passing grade in American history. Basically, it means Joanne won't be graduating with her class in June."

"I won't graduate?" The room seemed to whirl before Joanne's eyes. "No! I've got to!"

"Or . . ." Mrs. Kovelstein hesitated.

Joanne and her mother hung on that word. It seemed to linger in the air.

"Or we could try something else. But I hate to suggest it, because Joanne's shown difficulty in handling the study load she already has. Yet it's the only way."

Mrs. Palmer reached out and touched her

daughter reassuringly on the knee. "Whatever it is, we'll try it."

"Night classes," Ms. Kovelstein announced. "She can repeat American history again here with the juniors, and she can take civics and economics at night by special arrangement with the adult education system."

"Night classes?" repeated Joanne feebly.

"Yes. I have the schedule right here. Tuesdays and Thursdays, six-thirty to nine-thirty."

Three hours of class at a time? Joanne swallowed hard. She opened her mouth to protest, but nothing came out.

"That'll be fine," said Mrs. Palmer hurriedly. The reassuring hand tightened on Joanne's knee.

Ms. Kovelstein nodded briskly. "That's settled then. Joanne, I'll get your new schedule ready. You'll start on Monday."

"Yes, ma'am." Joanne sat still, then realized her mother was pulling her up by the elbow. Joanne grabbed her books and stood up.

As they walked down the corridor, Mrs. Palmer said, "It's all right, dear. I'll explain it to your father." She stopped in the hallway and looked straight into her daughter's eyes. "It's your last chance, Joanne. You know what you have to do." Mrs. Palmer didn't say another word, just continued to stand there looking at her.

Joanne thought of all the counseling sessions they had been to over the years. Her mother used to rant and rave at every bad report card, but now she just stood back and let Joanne accept the consequences, which was as it should be. The trouble was, Joanne was generally happy with things as they were. She didn't care if she never saw anything higher than a C on her report card. But not to graduate with her class—the thought made her tremble.

"I know, Mom," she said finally. "You're putting me back on curfew, huh?"

"That's right. Ten o'clock."

"Even Fridays and Saturdays?"

"Especially Fridays and Saturdays. You have been grounded, my dear."

Joanne wondered how she was going to get through the next five months without parties, without dances, without driving privileges, without dates—and most of all, without Rob.

She was really in big trouble, she told herself.

Chapter Two

"**Y**ou're kidding!" exclaimed Lynn over the phone, pausing to snap the rubber band on her retainer. "Grounded for the rest of the year? The whole rest of it?"

"Yeah." Joanne set the five-minute timer beside the telephone. The timer had been a concession also—if she didn't use it, her phone would be cut off. For five dollars, however, her younger brother, Paul, had done something to it so that it actually ticked off ten minutes. So far, at least, her mother hadn't caught on. "Grounded until graduation." *If I graduate,* she added silently. She hadn't told Lynn that part— she still had trouble believing it herself.

"Wow." There was silence as Lynn reflected.

Then she said, "It's a good thing you don't have Rob to worry about."

"What do you mean?"

"Well, now you couldn't go out with him, anyway."

"I'd find a way around it, if he asked me out. I'd never turn him down."

Joanne could hear Lynn's exasperated sigh. "Rob's not that great a prize, Joanne."

"Oh, Lynn, you just don't know how I feel about him. I've got to get him back."

"I still think you're wasting your time," Lynn said, snapping her rubber band. Joanne wondered how it could be so loud over the phone; she barely noticed it when Lynn snapped it at lunch. "But if you want, I'll try to come up with a plan."

"Hey, wait a minute—no more plans or systems. That's what got me here in the first place."

"What are you talking about?"

"Someone I know told me that C is always the best answer on a multiple-choice exam."

"Oh, jeez," Lynn said. "You didn't do that, did you, Joanne? Mark every answer C?"

"Sure."

Dead silence. Then Lynn said very quietly, "Remember, I told you to read the question first, and if you didn't have the slightest idea what the answer was, *then* put down C. I didn't say mark *everything* C."

"Now you tell me."

12

Both reflected in silence on the horror of what Joanne had done.

"Oh, well," said Lynn, "it's too late now. You'll do better this time. Third time's the charm."

"It better be. I'm sick and tired of the Civil War."

"Think of how the Confederates felt." The band snapped again. "There's got to be some good coming out of this somehow."

Joanne looked at the timer. Her "five" minutes were almost up.

To change the subject, Lynn asked, "Who do you want to do on Monday?"

Because she didn't want to be bugged, Joanne answered quickly, "Bette Midler." She knew Lynn hated her.

"Gross. You're on your own."

Good, thought Joanne. The way she felt, she didn't want to be anybody—especially herself. She sighed heavily. "If only Rob—"

"Forget Rob," Lynn interrupted. "Anyway, did you get your new schedule worked out? Maybe you won't have to look at him anymore."

"Ms. Kovelstein called up. I still have PE and Spanish with you—which means, unfortunately, I have Spanish with Rob, too. But my study hall has been changed, and I'm not in his English class anymore—maybe I can start concentrating now. The only class that fit my schedule instead of English was journalism."

"Really? That doesn't sound so bad."

"Except that part of the course requirement for journalism is writing for the *Trailblazer*. Ugh!"

"Oh, Joanne." Lynn said sighing. "Don't be so negative. It could be worse."

"Oh, come on. Grounded for the rest of the year. No car. No boyfriend. This is the worst thing that's ever happened to me." The timer sounded. "Gotta go."

Lynn's voice sounded far away. "OK, but don't do anything drastic. I'll think of something."

Her friend probably would. Lynn had more ways of beating the system than anyone she knew. Joanne hung up slowly, picked up the timer, and dropped it in the little drawer of the telephone desk. With any luck, it would break and take her mother two weeks to replace.

As if on cue, Paul appeared at the den door, his fourteen-year-old grin as mischievous as ever. "For another five dollars, I can fix that timer so you'll get twenty minutes instead of ten."

"Forget it," Joanne told him. "Mom's not *that* absentminded. Besides, I'd have to borrow the money from you to pay you."

He shrugged. "For a little interest, say thirty percent, that could be arranged."

Paul disappeared when she threw the telephone note pad at him. She stared down the hallway, wondering how she could get rid of her bratty little brother. If only there were a club like AA, called Younger Brothers Anonymous. Lynn would probably join—she had an obnoxious younger sister. Better make that Younger *Siblings* Anonymous, Joanne thought.

But, on the other hand, if Paul could arrange for Rob to come back to her . . .

Chapter Three

Joanne woke up on Monday morning with a sore throat. She lay in bed feeling cranky and hot and dry, wondering if she were sick or if her mom had just left the heat on all night. She tried swallowing—her throat was tight. But she did feel it would be relieved if she had something soothing to drink, such as peppermint tea.

Outside her closed bedroom door, she could hear someone padding down the hall. She opened her mouth to call out—in case it was her mom—then she shut it quickly. If she had to ask for a second opinion, she probably wasn't that sick, she thought.

No, she was just nervous. She recognized the feeling from the times she had to take exams.

Taking a deep breath, Joanne tried to escape down into her bed, but all she could think of was the horror that faced her. Another semester of history! She closed her eyes. It was still early. Maybe she could get some more sleep, and everything would disappear.

But there was a rap on the door then, and Paul's changing voice tried a whisper. "Mom says if you get up now, you'll have time for french toast. Otherwise, it's cold cereal."

"Oh, go away! Just leave me alone." Joanne put the pillow over her face, shutting out the morning light.

"Oh, yeah?" Her little brother sounded vaguely interested. "Doing Greta Garbo today? It's 'I vant to be ah-lone,' " he corrected. The hall floorboards creaked as he moved away from the door. Joanne could hear Paul laugh.

The pillow slid off her face. That settled it. She got out of bed and peered into the tarnished mirror of the antique dresser that sat in the corner of her room. Its silvered surface was so old, she found it hard to see herself. She was always vaguely blurred. The mirror was slightly warped, too, so that the face staring back at her had a hazy, softened appearance.

It was the first day of her new schedule, and the more she thought about it, the more she dreaded it. She was most nervous about journalism, for she hated writing. In fact, she had parted with some of her hard-earned allowance last week to get Paul to write her Christmas thank-you notes.

Imagining what her first assignment would be, she stood at the mirror, pretending to jot down notes on an imaginary pad. "Tell me, sir, what were your first thoughts when you saw the earthquake take your wife and children and family dog right in front of your eyes?"

The mirror said nothing, but the oval face inside squeezed out a frown. "Why . . . I thought of all the insurance I had on them! I'm rich!" Joanne laughed as she reached for her robe. Maybe there was a way to make the class more tolerable somehow.

By the time she had showered and blow-dried her hair, Joanne had decided to become Barbara Walters for the day. Her air of sophistication and authority would be the perfect front for journalism class. And, she rationalized, it might even help her get through history, too.

Mrs. Palmer's eyebrows went up when Joanne came downstairs wearing a brown skirt, soft beige blouse, blazer, and brown heels and sat down at the kitchen table.

"It's nice to see your eyes again," her mother said as she leaned over to pour Joanne a cup of tea. "Why don't you get your hair cut short?"

"That's the trouble with hair. I can get it cut short, but I can't get it cut long. Suppose I change my mind after it's too late? Mom, where's

Dad this morning?" Joanne added, changing the subject.

"He had to leave early."

"Work, huh," Joanne grumbled. "What a drag."

"So that's why we all got french toast," Paul said. "You had to get up early anyway."

Mrs. Palmer smiled. One side of her mouth turned up higher than the other, and Joanne thought it made her mother look tired. "I guess that's why," Mrs. Palmer answered, sitting down with her tea in front of her. "You do look nice, Joanne."

"Yeah," commented Paul. "I think she wants to impress her new history teacher."

"That's enough, Paul."

"I heard her telling Lynn. He's also the soccer coach—and soooo gorgeous."

"That's *enough*, Paul."

"Yeah," Joanne retorted. "We can't all be obnoxious geniuses." She tucked the tie on her blouse inside the collar so she couldn't drip syrup on it. "I'm so glad you've got Mr. Sheldon this year—you deserve each other."

"That's enough, you two." Mrs. Palmer removed the plate of french toast from Paul's hand and passed it to Joanne. Paul looked as if he were considering another remark, but after a look from their mother, he lowered his face and began eating.

Watching Paul eat was like watching a trash

20

compactor work, Joanne decided. She moved slightly in her chair so she couldn't see him.

"I'll drive you to school today," Mrs. Palmer said to them. "And Joanne"—she paused as she stood up—"don't waste too much time with Lynn after school. You've got a schedule to follow now."

Joanne shot Paul a look that was guaranteed to kill any smart-aleck remarks he might have thought about making. Paul's eyes widened innocently. Then, with his mouth full of food, he dropped his jaw and stuck his tongue out at her.

Lynn arrived at school a few minutes after Joanne. She paused to examine her friend beside their adjacent lockers, her expression showing amazement. "That don't look like any 'Divine Miss M' I've ever seen," she said, fracturing her grammar on purpose.

"It's not." Joanne was fishing through the tangle of books and papers in her locker. Carefully she pushed aside the stack of Rob's notes in order to reach her books. No one could say the tall, dark boy was eloquent, but he had been quite attentive during the time they had dated. Two or three times a week she had been able to count on finding a note pushed through the vents of her locker.

Lynn stepped back. She was wearing her blond hair in a curled ponytail, and she had

21

cuffed her jeans—evidently doing Olivia Newton-John for the day. "Let me see . . . I think I know . . ." she murmured, eyeing Joanne.

Joanne put on a somber expression and did her best impression of Gilda Radner doing the famous reporter.

"Barbara Walters!" Lynn shouted. "That's perfect. Good luck on the *Trailblazer*."

"I'll need it."

Lynn shrugged. "Come on, we're going to be late."

"Mrs. Herbert won't mind." Joanne found her Spanish book and business machines notebook and tucked them under her elbow.

As she walked into her senior Spanish class, the first person Joanne saw was Rob—and the second person she saw was Christina Roe, co-head of the songleaders and a class beauty. The blond was sitting at the desk next to Rob's, her head pressed close to his. Joanne gasped. Was Christina the reason Rob had dumped her?

Joanne was so shocked she tripped over a chair standing in the corner. As heads turned, she blushed, sidled up to the nearest desk, and sat down awkwardly. Rob watched her for a long minute, smiling. Christina smiled, too, before she turned her attention back to Rob. Nothing could cut as deep as that smile, Joanne thought, as she slid her books under her seat.

She whispered to Lynn, "For this you made me live through the weekend?"

Joanne continued to dwell on Rob and Christina until fourth period when she had to trot across the campus to journalism class.

The high school was old. It had been built in the twenties and had been added onto as the city and its population had grown. The main building had three floors with a one-story wing attached to it. Three "temporary" Quonset huts sat in part of the faculty parking lot. A new four-story tower dominated the far corner of the campus along with an even newer gym and half-stadium. The junior high school was adjacent to the gym.

Joanne's new schedule had her running all over the campus. She thought that because of it, she could probably lose several pounds before graduation. As Lynn had said, *some* good had to come out of it.

The journalism class was in a room on the open end of the wing. That made it convenient for the students who worked extra hours and tramped in and out. Joanne bumped into one of them, the editor of the *Trailblazer*, Simone Collier, on her way to class. Joanne swore that Simone never ate lunch and rarely went home for dinner. She could always be seen loping in and out of the wing, her long legs carrying her effortlessly. *Now there is someone who could do a good Brooke Shields*, Joanne reflected.

23

The journalism room was cluttered, with desks pulled in every direction, as if their occupants had sat in small groups collaborating on stories. The walls, except for the bank of windows, were covered with cork bulletin boards, which, in turn, were covered with newsprint. Some articles were from the *Trailblazer*, and the remainder were from newspapers all over the world.

At the end of the room, on either side of Mrs. Stickney's desk and green chalkboard, were two doors. Beyond, Joanne could see an even more cluttered room. It looked like an old science lab someone had filled with used typewriters and drafting tables. Most of the students were gathered in there.

Joanne sat down at the first empty desk she came to. The green chalkboard in the inner room was covered with spidery printing—Mrs. Stickney's, she supposed. It read: "INVERTED PYRAMID—Who, what, when, where, why, and sometimes how." It looked as if Mrs. Stickney had written it the first day she had begun teaching at Fremont High some twenty-five years before and had never erased it.

Piling her books at her elbow, Joanne reflected that Barbara Walters had probably started out in some journalism class like this—broadcast journalists usually did. She tilted her head back a little, thinking. . . .

"Joanne Palmer?"

She started, and her elbow crashed into the books. Mrs. Stickney caught them and righted them.

"Daydreaming?" she asked, smiling.

"Yes. Ah, no, I mean—" Joanne swiveled in the chair to see Mrs. Stickney standing beside her. The journalism teacher reminded her of an apple doll—she had bright red cheeks, a wrinkled face, and a halo of blue-gray hair. She was quite short and very thin. Spry was the word, although Mrs. Stickney wasn't really old. Silver-rimmed glasses hung around her neck on a silver chain, and a pencil was pushed behind her right ear. Joanne also noticed she had ink stains on her fingers.

"Welcome. I'm glad we have a few minutes to talk." Mrs. Stickney eased into the desk opposite her. "Now, Joanne, as you know you must be an A or B student in English to take journalism. The school has compromised somewhat by allowing you to come in here."

"It's—" Joanne began to say that it was the only thing that fit in her schedule, but Mrs. Stickney raised a hand and interrupted.

"I know. It must be awfully important to you. All we can hope is that you will enjoy being part of the staff. Maybe you can earn a by-line or two before the year is out. Most of my students start taking journalism classes as soon as they can. All of our editors have been on the staff since their sophomore or junior years."

Joanne smiled, a gracious Barbara Walters smile, unwilling to disillusion the older woman. "I can certainly understand that."

"Good."

Mrs. Stickney sprang out of her chair and crossed to the front of the room, calling the class to order. Joanne crossed her legs, smoothing down her skirt carefully, and began to worry all over again. If journalism was as rough a course as Mrs. Stickney hinted at, she'd be doomed to be a high-school student forever.

"Get out your paper and pencils," Mrs. Stickney said to the class. "In about five minutes the student body president, Cliff Wright, will be here. He has agreed to be the subject of a *'Blazer* article. Since this is his first year in school and his victory was such an upset in the election, we thought Fremont students would want to know more about him and how he's handling his position. This will be a collective interview done under the editorial 'we.' "

"What do you mean by that?" A younger boy stuck up a hand to legalize the question he'd blurted out.

"Glad you asked. Instead of questions posed by individuals, we'll show the interview as a staff effort. For example. ' "How do you like California?" asked the *Trailblazer.*' "

Stifling a yawn, Joanne rummaged around in her purse for a pencil. The interview sounded deadly dull.

Her head was down, and she was doo-dling Rob's name on her note pad when the door opened. She stopped and stared along with everyone else.

Joanne had seen Cliff Wright before, but he had a commanding presence that made her want to take a closer look. He wasn't nearly so good-looking as Rob, but he wasn't bad. She thought the wide, crooked smile he flashed when he introduced himself to Mrs. Stickney was sort of cute. His hair was golden brown, and his eyes were a soft, smoky color.

The teacher shook his hand briskly, obvi-ously impressed with the senior boy. "Thank you for coming, Cliff."

"No problem," he said, taking a seat on the edge of Mrs. Stickney's desk. "Questions, anyone?"

Joanne groaned inwardly. Her mind grew foggy, and the sounds in the room retreated until she could barely hear anything specific. She did manage to write down the questions and Cliff's polite, though noncommittal, an-swers automatically, not really listening. If dull was deadly, Cliff was getting a fatal dose from these cub reporters.

Barbara Walters, though, had an intimate way of leaning forward and asking something sincerely, asking something so different from what her subject thought she was going to ask that the person was usually caught off guard, saying things he or she might not otherwise reveal.

Joanne closed her eyes and pictured Barbara. That soft, educated voice saying . . .

The journalism room was dead quiet as Joanne, playing Barbara, asked her question.

"That's a tough question," he remarked. "Would you repeat it?"

Joanne had to think fast; she had been so busy concentrating on being Barbara Walters that she couldn't even remember what she had just asked. Momentarily she panicked. Then she automatically shifted back into her Barbara Walters pose and said, "Perhaps you wouldn't care to answer that right now."

"Oh, no." Cliff looked at her intensely. "I'd like to, but I'm not sure I'll give you the answer you want."

"Say what you want to say. No stock answers."

"All right then. What do I think I owe the students, the so-called little people, who elected me?" Cliff ran a hand through his hair. "I don't think I owe them anything, not in the sense of a political debt. After all, Fremont High isn't Tammany Hall. But I do think the office I hold has an obligation."

Joanne sat back, off the hook. Cliff turned from her to another girl as his reply sparked another question and another. Every now and then his eyes swept the room, and when his gaze met Joanne's, it lingered. She had made an impression on him, of that she was certain—but what kind?

Mrs. Stickney, who had been standing in the back, walked to her desk. She checked her watch. "We have time for just one more question."

"Barbara Walters" couldn't resist. She leaned forward one last time, and incredibly, Joanne heard herself asking, "Cliff . . . if you had just one thing you wanted us to rememeber about you, what would that be?"

Chapter Four

When Joanne emerged from the annex wing, she was pleasantly surprised to see Lynn sitting on an outdoor wooden table, two lunch trays steaming in front of her. In the space next to her was a waxed-paper package containing freshly baked chocolate chip cookies.

"Hey, neat!" Joanne grabbed the cookies first and munched one quickly. "I'm sorry I'm late," she added, her mouth full.

"It's all right. I didn't have anything better to do," Lynn said sarcastically.

But Joanne wasn't going to let Lynn make her feel upset. "Well, I *did*." She ate another cookie. "We did a group interview of Cliff Wright in journalism."

"The school president?" Lynn snapped her

retainer band, clearing it of cookie crumbs, and brightened a little. "What's he like?"

"He's all right. Nothing like Rob, though."

"We all know no one can match Rob," Lynn echoed dramatically.

Joanne pretended to ignore that and continued, "In any event, 'Barbara Walters' bowled him over."

"No, Joanne, you didn't!"

She nodded as she opened her purse and pulled out the money she owed Lynn for lunch. "Yeah, I did. I was just sitting there, going to sleep—I mean the interview was so boring—and Barbara took over."

"What happened?"

"Total success. Mrs. Stickney was pleased. She said we ought to end up with a good, in-depth portrait when we get done with it." Joanne sighed as the realization of what she had done settled in. "I hope nothing like that happens again. I don't think I can keep doing Barbara for an entire semester."

Lynn nodded, then looked at her friend strangely. "You didn't ask him if he was sexy, did you?"

"Lynn!" Joanne cried. "I'm not *that* stupid." She looked at the food on her tray. "Yech! What is this, anyway?"

Lynn leaned over for a closer look. "Meatballs and gravy over rice, I think. Those extra things might be mushrooms."

"Don't tell me any more. I don't want to know!" Dramatically Joanne plunged her fork in and took a bite.

A shadow fell across Joanne's tray. She twisted around and looked into Rob's dazzling, white-toothed smile. His blue-black hair glistened in the hazy sunshine, and he squinted a little— blue eyes crinkling at the edges. Joanne's heart did a quivery dance.

"Hi, Joanne," he said.

Lynn said, "Hi, Rob."

"Hi," he said absently.

"Sit down with us," Joanne said. "I haven't talked to you in a long time."

He shifted his notebook from one hand to the other. "No, thanks, Jo. I'm meeting Christina. I just wanted to explain what you saw in Spanish this morning. It must have been a surprise for you."

"That's all right, Rob. I can handle it," Joanne said, hoping "Barbara's" sophistication might rub off on her.

"I'm glad you understand," Rob said, peering around the tables. "Saves me the trouble of making a speech. Well, I've got to go. Be seeing you." He sauntered off.

Lynn sighed. "The nerve! He's got to rub it in, doesn't he?"

"Poor Rob," Joanne replied gallantly. "Once Christina's sunk her claws into him, he'll be roasted alive for even talking to another girl."

"It'll serve him right," Lynn muttered. "Stop wasting time on that jerk. He doesn't deserve you."

"Oh, don't be so hard on him." Joanne felt the need to defend her ex-boyfriend. Lynn, she thought, just didn't understand the way things were between them. "Rob's not the type to be taken in by a phony. I guarantee it won't last."

"So what else happened in journalism?" Lynn asked airily, wanting to change the subject. But then she interrupted herself. "Speaking of hunks—"

"We weren't."

Joanne watched as Lynn stared longingly at Cliff Wright walking across the grounds. Lynn waited until he was past before she repeated her question.

"I told you already," Joanne answered impatiently. "The interview took up the entire period." She didn't want to admit it to Lynn, but the sight of Cliff Wright unnerved her. She wasn't sure why.

Lynn stood up, picked up her tray, and left lunch early to wash out her retainer. She waved goodbye and wobbled off, her Olivia Newton-John ponytail bouncing behind her.

Joanne started to stand up and yell after her. She'd forgotten to tell Lynn she couldn't have lunch with her every other Thursday because of the paper deadline. But Lynn was already too far away, so Joanne sat down. She could tell her another time. She barely had time to finish her lunch before the bell rang.

Joanne's history class was in the new tower on the third floor, and she was out of breath by the time she got there. Facing the door, she paused to inhale—once to catch her breath and once to summon up her nerve.

She wrinkled her nose. Beyond that door were about thirty inferior people she would have to sit with for the rest of the year. Juniors. Steeling herself, she followed the next group of kids inside.

She knew only one of them, a redhead, whom she'd just met in her journalism class. His name was Ken Winters, and he was into photography.

The door slammed shut as the bell rang. The teacher bounded in, looking as if he were chasing a soccer ball. A few of the girls rolled their eyes at each other.

Mr. Broadhurst was short and chunky. He wore his PE uniform—gym shorts, rugby shirt, and whistle around his neck—having decided evidently that this history class was not worth changing his clothes for. His shorts showed off heavily muscled legs and a deep tan, and his wavy, brown hair brushed the top of his collar. The thump he made sitting down in the teacher's swivel chair brought everyone not already staring to attention.

"Hi!" He waved a hand at them. "I have some good news and some bad news for you today."

Someone in the back groaned. He laughed. "I know. What's the good news? The good news is, the new textbooks still haven't come in. And it looks as if it's going to be a few more days till they do."

The class cheered.

Broadhurst hushed them. "The bad news is, I have an assignment for you, anyway. I want a short essay on your thoughts about the founding fathers. Now you're free to go to the library, or wherever you want to go, to do your writing, but don't make a fuss, or we'll all be in trouble. I hope"—he spread both hands as he rocked back in his chair—"we'll have the books later this week. Otherwise, we'll be reading each other's works."

With all the noise and speed of a retreating army, the juniors fled the class. Though she sat near the front, Joanne was caught in the crush and was one of the last to get out.

She made her way down the stairs and across the lawn to the first-floor library in the main building, and she slipped into the last unoccupied carrel. To her chagrin, who should be seated right next to her but Christina—Joanne couldn't have mistaken those golden blond curls anywhere. Quietly she sat down, hoping her neighbor wouldn't look up.

Luck wasn't with her. "Hi, Joanne," Christina said in her best syrupy-sweet voice. "What brings you down here?"

"A history report," she answered, hoping that would be the end of it.

"Hmm, history," Christina mused. "You're repeating that this semester, aren't you?"

"Yes," Joanne said, blushing. "How'd you find out?"

"I have my ways."

Joanne remembered that Christina worked in the principal's office and figured somehow she had gotten access to her file there. The sneak . . . she'd probably told Rob, too, if not the rest of the school as well. "Anyway, it's not so bad. I've got Broadhurst, and he seems like a fair enough guy."

"Good luck," Christina said.

"Thanks," Joanne answered, surprised that Christina would wish her well for anything. She was just about to open her notebook when Christina added, "Oh, by the way, Joanne, who's your date for the Valentine's Day dance?"

Joanne shivered in spite of herself. She shrugged. "It's still early—I haven't made up my mind."

"I suppose you heard about Rob and me. I just wanted to let you know he's already asked me."

Joanne felt her stomach tighten. "He has?"

she said, fighting back her tears. "Well, I hope you two have a good time."

Christina's blue eyes widened, and she smiled insincerely. "I'm so glad you're a good loser, Joanne." She turned back to her carrel.

Joanne clenched a fist to keep from throwing a book at her. She made herself relax, one finger at a time. She wasn't going to lie down and let Christina dance all over her. She would get Rob away from her somehow, curfew or not!

Furious with Christina, she let out her frustration by writing an angry paper about her feelings on history—it was people and *not dates* that were important. It did nothing to help her get Rob back, but it did make her feel better.

Joanne finished the last paragraph as the bell rang for last period. She had lucked out on her new schedule as far as PE was concerned. There was nothing she hated more than being stuck with PE in the middle of the day, showering and trying to reassemble herself to get to another class on time. With PE last period, she could take her time.

Lynn was dressed in her gym shorts and T-shirt and out on the gym floor by the time Joanne arrived. Mrs. Cochran, the gym teacher, made them run laps, so it was between puffs that Joanne told her friend about her run-in with Christina. Lynn, too out of shape to talk back, merely rolled her eyes in amazement.

Joanne sat on a wooden bench after she

dressed, waiting for Lynn, who was the last one out of the showers as usual. The musty, damp smell of the girls' locker room surrounded her. She balanced her journalism notebook on her lap and didn't notice when Lynn stood over her at last.

"What've you got there?"

"Huh?" Joanne looked up. "Oh, it's a journalism assignment. It's due Friday."

"What's your hurry?" Lynn pulled her sweater over her shirt and tugged her ponytail into place. "You never get anything done early."

Joanne shrugged as she put away her notebook. "It's an idea I had. You know how it is, if you don't write it down, you forget it." She stood up and put on her blazer. "Are you ready to go yet?" She checked her watch. "School was out ten minutes ago."

"So c'mon then." Her friend grabbed her by the elbow and towed her out of the gym as if Joanne were the slow one.

An unusually chilly wind urged them to walk briskly. From the look of the sky, Joanne didn't think it would rain, but she turned the collar on her jacket up, anyway.

Lynn stopped. "You taking all those books home?"

"Got to. Mom says I have to start a homework schedule."

"Again?"

"Yeah, again."

Lynn shrugged. "It didn't work last time. I don't know what makes her think it's going to work now." She snapped her retainer band.

"Hey!" Joanne felt insulted. "It's not Mom's fault, you know. I asked for it. Too much partying. I'm just not interested in this school stuff, that's all. And quit fooling around with your retainer, will you?"

Lynn's eyebrows arched up a bit. "Touchy, touchy, touchy! OK, I'm sorry about your mom. Still upset about Christina?"

"No," Joanne lied. She turned and watched the diamond patterns of the chain-link fence change into new shapes as she passed them. She could hear the shouts and cries of the varsity baseball team, out for their preseason practice, but she didn't look back to see them.

Lynn read her thoughts. "Rob was made captain of the team this year."

"Who told you?"

"Brad. He also said—well, never mind." Lynn leaned her face over and rubbed her nose on the cuff of her sweater. "This kind of weather always makes my nose itch."

"Forget your nose! What else did he say?"

"That Rob told him he was thinking of going one on one with Christina."

"Going steady already?" Joanne felt the color drain from her face. She knew if she looked in a mirror, her skin would be dead white.

Lynn laughed. "Jeez, you sound so old-fashioned."

"Different name, same game," Joanne retorted defensively. "We've got to plan something now. The Valentine's Day dance is coming up, and I don't have a date. I haven't missed a dance yet, and I don't intend to start now."

"You also don't have permission to go."

"I'll think of something!"

"Yeah, well . . ." Lynn shifted her notebook from one hip to the other as she walked. "A date I can get you."

"I don't want just any date. I want Rob. I've got to get him away from that girl."

Lynn pulled at her band with a fingernail, saw the scowl on Joanne's face, changed her mind, and relaxed the band without a sound. "Well, it won't be easy. Christina can play mean if she wants. Somehow we'll have to get him to pay attention to you again."

"Yeah, but how?"

"How about becoming a star reporter? He's always been impressed by prestige."

"You've got to be kidding! It was fun today—that much I'll admit—but I still hate to write. Besides, there's too long a line in front of me. If I get one by-line this semester it'll be a lot."

"I've got it," Lynn said after a moment's thought. "You know that night class you've got to take?"

"Two classes, Lynn. Two."

"Even better."

"How can you say that?"

"Easy. Boys, Joanne—*older* boys. College-age boys. Think about the possibilities."

Lynn might have something, Joanne thought. Rob was a lot of things, all good and glorious, but he also had a tremendous ego. He would like the idea of stealing her away from a college boy, *if* she could manage to be dating one. Or even if she and Lynn could arrange it so it *looked* as if she were dating one.

"When's your first class?" Lynn interrupted her thoughts.

"Tomorrow night."

"Your mom driving you?"

"She or Dad."

"Well, get one of them to take you early. Tell them you want enough time to locate the class, et cetera. Then—we'll just have to sweep somebody off his feet."

"But who?"

"That's the question. Who?" Lynn snapped her band this time, but Joanne didn't even hear it as she lowered her head, deep in thought.

Chapter Five

The following night Joanne made a face at her mirror as she got ready for dinner and her night class. Who could she pretend to be for night school? It had to be someone who was brash enough and entrancing enough to sweep a college man off his feet. She tilted her face one way and then another. Barbra Streisand might do it, but she didn't feel like doing Streisand. It took too much out of her.

Joanne pulled her hairbrush through her wavy brown hair. Rainy California winters always dulled the color. If it were spring, she could put lemon juice on it and streak it a little, but in winter she couldn't do anything to liven it up. Sometimes she felt as if she were going to merge into a mass of dark brown hair and disappear forever. If only she had honey-colored hair like Lynn or Christina.

Someone ran down the hallway outside her door and then ran down the stairs. From the vibration she knew it had to be Paul, and that meant it had to be dinner time. Hurriedly, Joanne dropped her brush, made one last face at the mirror, and headed for the dinner table.

Her father was sitting at the head of the table, absently reading a paper as Paul tried to finish setting plates around him. From the far-away look on his face, Joanne knew that he wasn't really reading but thinking of something else. Problem solving, he called it. Taking a deep breath, she sat down and noticed how the dining-room light reflected off her father's balding head. Forty and balding and dull as could be, she thought to herself. She loved her father, but Mr. Excitement he wasn't.

He folded the paper over his lap like a napkin when she sat down. "I'll drive you tonight, Joanne, and your mother will pick you up."

"OK." She rearranged her knife and fork. Paul never could get all four place settings perfect, though usually hers was messed up more than anyone else's.

"Dad."

"Hmm, baby," he said, staring at his lap.

"I'm sorry about the night classes and all." Her father hadn't mentioned anything about her situation, and she wondered what her

44

mother had said to him to hold him back. Normally he blew his stack at her about her grades.

Mr. Palmer stared at his daughter and answered slowly, "I'm sorry, too, baby. I always thought you took after me." He didn't see her wince. "In any case, you're smart enough to get through. It's something you're going to have to work out for yourself. You've backed yourself into a corner with an awful lot of work this semester."

"I know, Dad." She took a vegetable bowl from her mother.

The remark seemed to remind him of something as he looked up quickly at his wife. "Hon, I'll be home late tonight, and you better not count on me for dinner most of the rest of the week."

Susan Palmer sat down heavily. "All right. What's up?"

Joanne and Paul dished out servings for themselves quietly, listening to every word. Ever since their dad had decided to open his own accounting business, he had been working extremely long hours.

"John Fallworth's been called in for an audit. I'm going to have to get things straightened out as much as I can before he meets with the IRS."

"Are you going in with him?" Paul asked avidly, fork in midair.

"No. I wasn't his accountant then, and I didn't prepare the return. What he needs is a

45

tax lawyer, I suspect." Fred Palmer added hastily, as though he had just realized he was talking to his children and not his peers, "Don't let that get around."

"It must be fun."

"Fun?" Everyone echoed, and Joanne felt the stares of her family.

"Well, you know, Mr. Fallworth is pretty wealthy, and he's always going off here and there. Just reading his expense account must be interesting—like peeping in on his private life. Dinner at Le Chateau, jets to Washington, all that."

"That's not funny, Joanne," said her dad.

"I mean it," Joanne said, defending herself. "I'll bet he does a lot of interesting stuff."

"A client's business affairs aren't meant to substitute for 'Fantasy Island.' They're meant to be private."

"Now, Fred," her mother said soothingly, "I can see what Joanne means."

"Well, I can't. Now hurry up, or we'll both be late." He attacked his fried chicken with a vengeance and pointedly changed the subject.

Joanne finished the meal in silence except for a brief argument with Paul over who got the last wing. She won after she accused him of always hogging all the white meat.

Paul sat back in mock horror, putting his hand on his chest. *"Moi?"* he exclaimed.

"Yes, you." Joanne stabbed the wing and

flipped it onto her plate. Then an inspiration struck her. Thanks to Paul, she knew who she would be that night—Miss Piggy! *Perfect.* On impulse she leaned over and kissed her brother on the forehead.

"What's that for?"

"Oh, nothing." She finished quickly and hurried upstairs, yelling down at her mother, "I'll do the dishes when I get home!"

In her room she hurriedly got her notebooks together. She opened her jewelry box and pawed through the clutter until she found what she was looking for. She pinned a lacy ornament into her hair and put on a necklace with a rhinestone pendant. "There!" She said triumphantly as she looked in the mirror at herself.

"Moi?" she said and tossed her head, so that her dark hair bounced. "No, no, no, no. *Moi* am too modest! A pig of my talent cannot possibly be shy! Has anyone around here seen a little green frog?" Joanne finished as she and Miss Piggy thundered downstairs before they were late.

Fred Palmer pulled into the high-school parking lot. "Look for your mother here around nine-thirty. Do you have money to call home if class gets out early? I don't want you hanging around here in the dark."

"Moi will be fine." She kissed him good night. "And, Daddy—don't worry about Mr.

Fallworth. He'll be OK. You're a terrific account-ant."

"Huh? Oh." He looked pleased and faintly surprised. "Uh, thank you, Joanne." He put the car into gear and drove away slowly.

She watched him go and flipped her hair off her shoulder. "Well, Miss Piggy," she said aloud, "you and I have a new world to conquer!"

Joanne's class was meeting on the third floor of the tower, and she had plenty of time for exploring. All around the school there were night-class students milling around. Most of them were older—some even as old as her parents, she realized, heaving a huge sigh of disappointment. Lynn was going to be pretty disappointed, too, when she heard.

Joanne leaned against the concrete wall outside her classroom. It appeared as if Miss Piggy's talents were going to be totally wasted. Disgusted, she looked out the third-story window at the moths gathering around the outdoor lamps.

"Hi!"

Joanne looked up, startled. It was Ken Winters.

"What are you doing here?" Joanne asked.

The junior grinned. "I'm taking economics. What are you doing here?"

"Well—it's never too late to refine one's education."

"Oh." He blinked and looked questioningly at Joanne. "Well, I'm here because my parents won't let me take both photography and journalism unless I get my prerequisites out of the way. So I take night classes. Hey, you're in American history, too. What's the matter? You don't have enough credits to graduate?"

Joanne felt deflated. "Something like that," she muttered. "And if you tell anybody, I'll not only kill you, I'll break your camera."

He waved a hand. "Hey, it's all right with me. I won't tell. In fact, the information might come in handy." His grin widened. "Maybe you'd like to go out with me sometime."

"Date you? I'd sooner kiss a frog," Joanne retorted. She ducked inside the classroom as the buzzer sounded.

Joanne was a little disappointed as Ken Winters sat down in the chair next to hers. Didn't he get the hint?

She ignored him as the teacher, an ordinary, somewhat dumpy woman in jeans and a sweatshirt, quickly passed out sheets.

The name on the chalkboard read: Ms. Quincy. Joanne wondered if she knew *Ms.* Kovelstein. The thought pleased her, and she put her mind to reading the sheet of paper before she lost control. It listed the requirements for the course, the assignments, the dates they were due, as well as the test dates.

Ms. Quincy perched on top of the desk,

resting her sneakered feet on what was supposed to be the desk chair. She looked out over their heads.

"Class, this is economics. If your registration card says anything else, you're in the wrong room." She smiled. "This is your assignment sheet. If you lose it, you're in trouble. We're all adults here—" She paused, looking at Joanne and Ken, and corrected herself. "Well, we're mostly adults here. You are responsible for the material listed. Tests are indicated plainly, so it's your own fault if you get surprised."

Class time fled quickly for Joanne—the course wasn't half so dull as she had envisioned it. At break time she nearly got trampled by the stampede of frantic smokers; by the time she reached the hallway, it was hazy with clouds of smoke. Ken bolted off, saying something about looking for a Coke machine, and she was left alone.

She wandered down the hallway to get away from the smoke. Without warning, a tall figure sprang out in front of her, causing her to stumble back.

"Sorry!" The figure leaned toward her from the shadows, one hand held out.

Joanne clutched her notebook to her chest, heart thumping. She relaxed as Cliff Wright's concerned face became recognizable. "Oh, hi, Cliff."

He looked anxious. "I didn't mean to frighten

you. You looked like you were a million miles away."

"Frighten *moi*? Not possible. I'm fine, really."

"By the way, we haven't had a proper introduction. Your name is Joanne Palmer, isn't it?"

"But of course!" she exclaimed.

"I didn't get a chance yesterday to thank you for your insightful questions."

"Thank me?" Surprised, Joanne looked up—straight into Cliff's twinkling gray eyes.

He nodded. "Until you stepped in, I was getting bored up there."

In spite of herself, Joanne smiled. "Me, too." Then quickly she returned to her Miss Piggy pose. "I don't have time for such silly people," she said, waving her hands.

Cliff smiled, and there was something about the way his face lit up that Joanne found appealing. He took her elbow and steered her down the walkway toward the classrooms. "You ought to stay with the crowd," he told her. "There have been some problems on the campus at night."

"Don't tell my parents. They'll never let me come."

He shrugged. "It's all right if you have the sense to stay with the crowd. What parking lot are you in?"

"I don't have a car. My mom's picking me up in the east lot."

"I'm parked there. I'll wait for you later, if you want."

"You don't need to do that," Joanne told him.

The smile warmed his face again. "Call it fulfilling an obligation to one of the 'little people' who voted for me," he answered slowly.

Joanne laughed in spite of herself. "What makes you so sure I voted for you?"

"Another one of your pointed questions. I shouldn't have walked into that one." Cliff slowed his long stride to match hers as they walked. "I'll counter with a pointed question of my own: What brings you here?"

"I have classes, twice a week."

He considered that. He had a slow, deliberate way of talking, as though he thought things over thoroughly first. "How do you have time for accelerated classes? The paper must really fill your schedule."

So he thought she was in the advanced college-level program for high-school students! Joanne opened her mouth, saying, "Oh, I'm not—" and shut it just as quickly. Why should she bother to correct a mistake like that? "I'm not an editor," she improvised. "This is my first go at journalism."

"Could have fooled me. You seem to have a flair for it."

If only he knew how she had faked her way through that interview! She looked at the thick bundle of spiral-backed notebooks under his arm and attempted to steer the conversation away from herself. "What are you taking?"

"Computer math. They have access to time at night."

Joanne grimaced unconsciously.

"Don't look so pained. It's rather fun. In my old school I learned how to do programs and all that as well."

"Interesting," Joanne said. "That was up in Washington, right?"

"Bellingham."

"What made you come here?"

"My mom. She and Dad got divorced last year, and she was looking for a place to start over."

"A lot of people come to California for that."

"Well, she's adjusted fine." Cliff stopped and leaned his lanky frame against the wall. "But I tell you, it's pretty hard to start your senior year in a new place."

"Being student body president must help," she said.

Cliff shook his head. "That was a real fluke. Lucky for me Fremont High is a hotbed of apathy. I was the only one running who really wanted the job. But it hasn't helped much. I've got high visibility but not much else."

The buzzer sounded, and Cliff straightened up. "I'm serious about walking you to the parking lot." He turned to head back to his class.

"Thanks," she called after him. "It's a deal."

As she slipped back into her classroom, she wondered if Lynn would consider the student-body president as good as a college man.

Chapter Six

For the third day in a row, Joanne had to endure the sight of Rob and Christina huddled together during Spanish class. Although she tried not to look, she couldn't avoid the couple in the row against the window, whispering and giggling and generally pretending the rest of the class didn't exist. It was enough to make a girl sick, Joanne thought.

Her new schedule had her going from Spanish to study hall. This one was monitored by Mr. Bostwick, who long ago had given up the idea that study hall was a place for work. By the time Joanne walked into the room, a few students were already perched around the middle-aged teacher's desk, ready for his daily jokefest.

Deciding she was not in the mood for

humor, Joanne took a seat in the back of the room. For once, she figured, she'd actually attempt to do her Spanish homework before begging Lynn for help. She was about halfway through the assignment when a long shadow crossed over her notepaper. She looked up into Cliff Wright's smiling face.

"Can I help you?" she asked.

Cliff took an adjacent seat. "I thought journalists were pros at grammar. It's 'May I help you,' I believe."

Ordinarily Joanne would have shot back a sarcastic word or two to someone who spoke to her like that. But there was something about Cliff's easygoing manner that stifled the biting words before they could come out. "What do you want?" was all she answered.

"I didn't mean to bother you," Cliff said, "but I'd had enough of the comedy workshop up there. Those jokes are older than the hills."

"Some people just don't have a sense of humor," Joanne said, keeping her eyes focused on her Spanish book. From the way she said it, it was unclear whether she meant Cliff or Mr. Bostwick. Even Joanne was unsure. All she knew was that Cliff had sparked a series of confusing feelings inside her that she didn't want to deal with.

"Did you get home all right last night?"

"Oh, sure. Thanks for walking me to the lot."

"That's OK." Cliff smiled.

Joanne eyed him curiously. "Say, what are you doing here anyway?"

"This is my study hall," he said.

"How come I haven't seen you around before?"

"Sometimes I use the period for student government work."

"Oh, I see," Joanne said, thinking.

"Joanne, I was wondering . . . If you're not doing anything this Saturday, would you like to go out with me?"

Joanne gulped. That was the last thing she expected him to say. "Gee, Cliff, I'd sure like to," she began, "but I've got a real heavy study load. I'm afraid I can't make it." At least, she thought, she was telling him the truth about the work.

"Maybe some other time, then," Cliff said, disappointed.

"Maybe," she said, smiling. "I'll let you know."

As Cliff ambled back to his desk, Joanne thought she might take Cliff up on his offer—when she knew Rob would be around to see them together.

If Joanne expected to use Cliff to make Rob jealous, it was going to take some doing. He wasn't in study hall for days, and Joanne couldn't find him around the campus. She was beginning to think he was merely a figment of her imagination until he popped up again at an all-school assembly the following Friday.

Dressed in a navy blue jacket and tie and sporting a new, trim haircut, Cliff looked as mature as any college boy Joanne had ever seen. He led the assembly in the Pledge of Allegiance and introduced the speaker, an officer from the Fremont Police Department, before taking a seat at the edge of the stage.

"He sure is impressive looking," she found herself whispering to Lynn.

"Officer McCormack?" her friend said incredulously.

"No, silly. Cliff Wright."

"Hmm, do I detect some interest here?" Lynn asked hopefully. "It's about time you got Rob off your brain."

"I haven't given up on Rob," Joanne explained. "I was just wondering what he would do if he saw me hanging out with Cliff."

"How are you going to manage that?"

"I'm not sure yet, but I'm positive Cliff will help me out. I think he likes me."

"So why don't you forget Rob and go out with Cliff?"

"I'll never stop loving Rob," Joanne insisted. "Cliff's just a friend."

"I think you're making a mistake, Joanne. Rob's getting tighter with Christina every day."

"You're wrong. It won't last once Rob gets reminded of the good times we had."

"Well, don't come to me for any ideas," Lynn responded. "You're on your own now, kid."

On the following Thursday afternoon Joanne sat in the journalism lab, absorbed in transcribing her handwritten notes to a typed form. Since there was no deadline that week, the other typewriters were silent. She was all alone.

She sat back in her chair, chewing on her pencil, finding it hard to concentrate her somewhat scattered thoughts. She was still in shock from having, earlier that day, earned her first A since second grade. What made it even more of surprise was that it was in history. When Mr. Broadhurst had returned the history papers written two weeks before, Joanne was thinking only about why he was wearing a coat and tie. The answer became obvious when he explained he'd been to the administration office trying to explain why it was difficult to teach class without books.

Then he announced the topic of the day's lecture—none other than the topic Joanne had written about. It was then that she looked down at her paper and noticed a red A. She felt it had to have been a mistake, but it was *her* name next to that A and *her* ideas Mr. Broadhurst was discussing. She spent the rest of the period in shock, hardly hearing the lecture.

"Thanks for your candid thoughts," Mr. Broadhurst told her afterward. "You gave me good material for today's discussion."

Joanne sucked on her pencil reflectively. The glow was fading slowly, but it was still there. She wanted to be able to do something similar in journalism, but she detested any writing that was scholarly or analytical. She just wanted to put her own thoughts down on paper, and she hoped she could get away with it in journalism.

Certainly she could get away with it in the article she was working on—a review of the play *Antigone* that the Drama Club was putting on in the Little Theater. She'd seen the dress rehearsal the day before with Lynn, who had to keep snapping her retainer bands to stay awake during the two-hour performance. It wasn't the liveliest play, Joanne had to agree, but she was impressed with the performances and the dedication of the crew members she'd seen working behind the scenes. Afterward, she had asked the drama teacher, Mr. Musselman, why he had selected a Greek play for production.

"What kind of answer do you want?" he had asked her.

"Whatever you want to say. I'm giving you a chance to defend your choice to the students."

She had listened carefully as Mr. Musselman told her of the need to expose young people to the classics. Writing down his answers furious-

, she had asked question after question about
he play, the cast, the choice of costumes and
cenery, surprising herself with the way the
uestions poured out of her mouth effortlessly,
s if she were a born drama critic.

She decided to get the piece done once and
or all. She knew her review wouldn't bring in
n audience—the play would already be closed
y the time the paper came out—but she wanted
o give the cast and crew credit for their efforts.
rowning, Joanne began to punch away furi-
usly on the old manual machine, the keys
ammering and producing vibrations all the
ay up her arms.

She had just corrected a mistake and put
he top on a bottle of correction fluid, when she
eard a familiar voice say, "Hi, Jo."

She gasped, dropping the bottle, which clat-
ered on the floor. Her pulse jumped as she
wiveled the chair around to face Rob.

He grinned, his smile bright against his
ear-round tan. He wore his baseball jersey under
is football letter sweater. His dark hair curled
round the sides of his cap.

"Oh, hi." Joanne returned his smile with
n unsteady one.

He walked over to where she was sitting.
How's it going? I just bumped into Simone,
nd she told me I'd find you here. I hear you've
ot a pretty full schedule these days."

"It's going OK. How are you? I heard you

made captain of the team. That's great. You be good at it."

He shrugged. "How do you like working o the paper?"

"It's terrific," she said, trying to impres him. "I'm working on an article right now."

"Really?" Rob snickered. "I'd have though it'd be a little too serious for you."

"Hey." She felt insulted, then remembere it was Rob she was talking to and backed down With her foot she tried to find the bottle sh had dropped. She quickly bent over and picke it up, but even so, when she sat back up, he face felt tomato red. "I'll have you know, Simon told me she considers me the 'Blazer's fastes rising star."

"I'm impressed," he said, in a way that to her he wasn't.

"And she's not the only person in this schoo who thinks I have just the proper level of ser ousness. The president of the student body doe too." She emphasized the last sentence.

"Cliff Wright?" Rob considered the possibi ity. "Well, good for you. I'm glad you're not spend ing all your time waiting around for me to mak up with you."

"*Moi?*" she said without much enthusiasm She could see she'd have to try a different tactic

"Yeah, I'm pretty tight with Christina now Let's be friends, though, OK?"

"I thought we always were," Joanne an

swered, though she wasn't quite sure what she meant by that.

"Listen, as long as you're here, I came by to find out who's going to be covering the games this season. You know?"

"No. Why do you ask?"

"It pays to know," he answered. "Could you find out for me?"

"Of course, Rob," she answered eagerly. "No problem."

"Well, see ya sometime." He waved and strolled off.

Joanne watched him leave, her heart giving a last odd thump before settling back into its regular rhythm. Despite what he said, she still hadn't given up hope he'd tire of Christina and come running back to her. In truth she couldn't imagine anyone putting up with Christina's demanding nature for long.

The following Thursday was deadline day at the *Trailblazer*. Large, blank double sheets of newsprint were everywhere as Simone and others adjusted their editorial pages. The *Trailblazer* was a small, offset paper with a front page, double inside page, and back page. Usually the front had "hard news," the inside contained sports, editorial issues, and letters, and the back, features. Joanne had always taken the paper for granted, but now she was amazed at all the energy that went into putting it out.

Mrs. Stickney patted Joanne on the shoulder as she rushed by. "Your article on *Antigone* was wonderful," she said. "I'm very pleased with your work." The woman smiled, crinkling her apple-colored cheeks.

"Wow. Uh, thanks," Joanne called after her as she scurried away into the classroom. She stayed in the lab, watching George Carruthers bend over a drafting board with a mock-up of the sports page.

One of the pictures before him showed Rob in his baseball uniform, smiling at the camera, surrounded by songleaders. Christina had her arms wrapped possessively around Rob. Joanne had to admit her rival looked stunning. The caption below read: BASEBALL SEASON TAKES OFF.

George pointed to it. "Nice shot, huh? A couple more like that and they'll have to get engaged."

Chills ran down her back. In spite of what Rob had said, in spite of the picture, in spite of all the evidence, she hadn't given up on him yet. She loved him too much. "What do you mean by that?"

George grunted. "Uh, well, I keep getting requests from Rob to take pictures of the two of them, and he wants copies. Anyhow, if this keeps up all semester, people are going to think they're pretty serious about one another. Power of the press, and all, y'know?"

"Yeah," she said under her breath. "Power

of the press," and turned away from the sports page before it made her ill.

George muttered, "Rob's really headed for trouble, though."

"What?" Joanne pivoted back to him.

He hesitated as though he weren't sure he should go on. "I hear he's been missing a lot of practices to be with her," he said at last. "The coach won't put up with that too much longer. Makes a good story, though."

Joanne bolted from the lab but was stopped by Simone, who ran into her by the classroom door. Joanne paused, sure that her face was still red with thoughts about Rob, but the tall girl didn't seem to notice.

Simone smiled. "That was a terrific piece you wrote on *Antigone*."

"Oh, thanks." Joanne stood there miserably, wanting to leave. At the moment, she couldn't care less about that dumb article.

The editor hesitated. "I—ah—wonder if you might like to cover an assignment for us next weekend? I don't know if we'll have room for it in the paper or not, but we need somebody to go."

"Sure," she answered automatically. "Uh, what is it?" she added as an afterthought.

"The county band and cheerleading competition at the junior college next Sunday. Our band is expected to do pretty well. I've got Ken lined up to take pictures."

"Will the pep squads be there, too?"

"The whole division."

The wheels inside Joanne's head began to spin. Rob was bound to be there to watch Christina compete. There had to be some way she could turn that situation to her advantage. . . .

Chapter Seven

Joanne paused at the top of the bleachers and looked out over the field.

Ken clicked his camera. "What kind of shots do you want me to take, Joanne?"

"The usual, I guess. Simone wants the teams posed with their trophies and ribbons if they get any. Maybe something different will happen."

"Nothing ever happens at these things." He dropped the camera back onto his chest and adjusted the strap around his neck.

Joanne shrugged as she sat down. Her green gabardine skirt rode up over her knees. Staring at it, she wondered if she'd made the right decision by "doing" Barbara Walters again. The skirt was awfully uncomfortable, and she was convinced she was going to snag her panty hose on the bleachers. But, she told herself, she was doing it because of Rob—and that made her feel better.

Joanne had done a lot of thinking since she had gotten the assignment. She remembered the remark Rob had made about her not being "serious" enough for journalism. This would be the perfect opportunity to prove him wrong. Dressed à la Barbara, she couldn't help but impress him with her professional look. And that, she reasoned, would certainly make her score higher in his eyes than flighty Christina in her silly songleader's outfit. Her dress and attitude had impressed her father enough for him to allow her to "fulfill her journalism assignment" by attending this event.

Looking disgusted, Ken scrambled down from the bleachers and loped off over the field. She watched him leave, glad to be alone for a moment.

Joanne braced her feet on the wooden-slat seat in front of her. Things just had to go her way with Rob. After all, she reasoned, it had been her lucky week. After Simone had given her the assignment, she had breezed into Broadhurst's history class, where she had had to write an essay on the topic of her choice. She had written about Lincoln's censorship of the news during the Civil War. It was a natural—Mrs. Stickney had just lectured on it. Broadhurst didn't tell them until they were done, and the papers turned in, that they had just had their first test of the semester. Joanne was sure she had done well on it.

That night she'd also taken her first test in economics. It was a multiple-choice one, and this time—much to her relief—she hadn't had to resort to Lynn's answering system. She was sure she had passed with flying colors.

So there was no doubt in her mind that after a week of terrific grades, she was due for some good news regarding her love life. Nobody, but nobody, could be better for her than Rob, and she was ready to make him see that.

By the time Ken came back and handed her a slightly warped wax cup full of diluted Coke, the bleachers around them were filling in with students and parents. Joanne caught a brief glimpse of Fremont's blue-and-gold as the band marched across the field to the warm-up area behind the bleachers on the other side.

Rob strolled in just before the judging began, with Christina clinging to his arm. The rest of Christina's squad surrounded the pair, waving their arms in welcome. From their actions, Joanne had the impression they had been worried Christina might not show up. Joanne watched with interest as the squad ran through a rough practice and then disappeared off the field until its turn to compete.

A few minutes later, a boy with long, thin legs took the seat next to Joanne.

"Hi, Joanne."

Joanne turned just as Cliff smiled. "Hi, Cliff. Glad you could make it." As part of her plan, Joanne had asked Cliff to join her on the pretext of commenting on the competition.

"Believe it or not, I would have been here anyway. I like to keep up with school activities. I miss not being able to participate in events like this. I was in the band at my old school."

"Really? What instrument?"

"I was the drum major. But Fremont's got a good one in Russ Vincent."

"I hadn't taken much notice of the band before today."

"I sort of feel an obligation to check out everything about Fremont. I've been impressed with the number of activities the school sponsors. There are some pretty interesting ones. And some interesting people—including some I'd like to get to know better." Joanne chose to ignore the obvious look in Cliff's eyes. She had enough trouble with one boy.

"Look, Cliff, the competition is starting. I've got to watch." She took out a pencil and note pad from her purse.

"Understood," he said. "Duty calls, I know."

The Fremont cheerleaders bounced on the field with enthusiasm. They led their famous "Rah, rah, ree, kick 'em in the knee; Rah, rah, rass, kick 'em in the other knee" cheer to the amusement of the stands and placed second in the overall competition, with a first for pep and energy.

The songleaders followed, led by Christina with her bouncy, short skirt and mane of fluffy, blond hair. But her enthusiasm couldn't make up for her lack of preparation. As the music started, she muffed the lead-off, and the whole routine got snarled up. The squad recovered, but it was obvious they were not functioning as a unit. Joanne saw Rob flex his shoulders, a gesture he made when he was angry about something. A disappointed Christina straggled off after her squad mates.

"Some song leader," Cliff muttered.

"Huh?" Joanne turned to look at him.

"A girl like Christina shouldn't be allowed to wear a Fremont uniform. She performed like she couldn't care less."

"I don't think she does," Joanne said. "But the songleaders have a lot of prestige in school. She'd never quit."

"Well, that weird Rob she hangs around with doesn't help any."

Joanne couldn't control herself. "Rob is anything but 'weird.' I'll have you know he is one of Fremont's best athletes. A real credit to the school."

"Excuse me," Cliff said contritely. "I guess I hit a sore point."

"I'll say." She stood up and looked for Ken, who was making his way to the field for a picture of the contestants. "I've got to go," she said, walking angrily away.

"I'm sorry," Cliff called after her. But Joanne didn't hear.

She waited for Ken in a comfortable, shady spot at the edge of the bleachers. Almost immediately the quiet of the spot was broken by the sound of angry voices. Curious, Joanne peered cautiously around the corner.

Rob was angrily confronting Christina, who stood with her face lowered, her pom-poms drooping from her hands.

"What kind of showing was that?" Rob demanded. "It's a good thing the whole school wasn't here. You really embarrassed us out there. What happened?"

She shrugged. "I'm sorry, Rob. I guess I missed too many practices, that's all. Don't you think I feel bad?"

"Feeling bad isn't enough. Do you know the *Trailblazer* is doing a write-up? I saw Joanne sitting in the stands with Cliff. It's going to be all over the school paper."

She looked up, retorting, "You can't have it both ways, Rob McAllister. If you want me to be good, then you can't expect me to cut squad practices to be with you. Besides, I'm not the only one who's not so hot on the field."

"What do you mean by that?" he asked angrily.

Christina backed up a step. "Oh, nothing.

Look, I'm upset about losing, too." She turned away from Rob for a moment as if thinking, then spun around as if struck with inspiration. "We can still use this to our advantage," she said, brightening. "This is what we'll do, and don't you dare mess up, Rob." She grabbed him by the elbow and pulled him away, and Joanne could no longer hear. But she could see him nod his head, as if in agreement.

Tears stinging her eyes, Joanne pulled back under the bleachers. For a moment Rob had been so mad at Christina, he seemed ready to dump her. But whatever Christina said to him changed his mind. Rob brushed past Joanne without seeing her and stopped to chat with another songleader, Cathy Turner. Joanne ducked back into the crowd, bumping unexpectedly into Ken. Coke sloshed out of his cup.

"Hey!" He wiped his jeans off. "What's the hurry?"

"Let's just get the dumb pictures and go."

Christina gave them a brittle smile as they approached. "Why, hello, Joanne. What are you doing here?"

"Uhhh—I was drafted to write up the competition," she said. She hung back as Ken first lined up the cheerleaders and then the songleaders for their group shots.

Rob strolled out of the shadows, his easygoing smile as brilliant as ever.

"How about a shot of the famous Fremont pyramid?" he suggested casually.

"Hey, neat," Ken answered. He started winding his camera for the next shot as the girls bounded into place. The pyramid was four rows high, with Christina posed triumphantly on top.

Ken aimed. Rob moved close to him as he got ready to snap. "Ho-o-l-d it!" Ken ordered.

But Rob edged even closer, causing Ken's elbow to wiggle as the shutter clicked. "Darn!"

"Sorry," Rob apologized. He moved away.

"That's all right." Ken shot him an odd look as he advanced the film. "Don't move, girls. I've got lots of film left!"

The girls on the bottom groaned a little. There was an imperceptible shift as the strain of holding their squad mates showed. As Joanne watched, a lump formed in her throat that wouldn't go away. She had no desire to see Christina featured so prominently in a photo, especially after her disastrous performance today. Behind her she could hear the strains of "Seventy-Six Trombones" as the Fremont band went through its final drill before competition. She ought to be out there, watching, she thought. At least that's what "Barbara" would have done.

A girl on the bottom moaned, her face dripping with perspiration. "Come on, guys. This is murder after competing all day."

Ken held up a hand. "Just one more shot,"

he told them as he focused his camera. "In case this one doesn't develop properly."

There was a ripple in the pyramid just then, and someone yelled, "Look out!" Joanne stepped back instinctively.

The pyramid toppled slowly, Christina falling from the top. Rob ran forward, and with a graceful half-somersault the songleader landed in his arms. The rest of the girls collapsed into giggles.

"Oh, Rob! I might have broken a leg or something!" Christina cried as she hugged him thankfully. Ken's camera continued to click away steadily.

The songleader turned to Joanne and grinned. "Some rescue, huh? That ought to look good in the paper."

Joanne could feel the heat of anger rise all the way to her scalp. "I doubt it, Christina," she said flatly.

Christina's smile faded. "What do you mean?" she said anxiously. "Ken, didn't you get a picture of it?"

"Sure!"

"Sensational! It's news, Joanne. Aren't you obligated to print the news?"

"Only when it's real," she retorted. "I'm a reporter, not a newsmaker."

Her hands on her hips, Christina challenged her, "Just what are you trying to say, Joanne?"

Joanne's heart thumped wildly. "All I have

to say is that you always do what you have to do to make yourself look good."

"You're just angry because Rob dumped you for me. Isn't that it?" She swung around to Rob. "You said Jo would do anything you asked her. Make her print that picture and story."

He cleared his throat uneasily. Joanne felt the stares of everyone on her. "Jo, I—" He stopped.

She shook her head. "I won't do it." The lump in her throat began to rise, and she bolted away.

"Quit following Rob around like a sick puppy dog!"

Joanne's eyes stung, and she ran blindly away.

"Hey! Wait for me," Ken shouted after her.

Joanne rubbed her hand across her face, fiercely blotting out her tears. She looked up at the sound of a whistle. The Fremont Marching Band was thundering down the field with the drum major striding in front. He blew the whistle again and turned smartly to the right. But the blue-and-gold turned smartly to its left.

"Move, Joanne!" cried Ken. "You're going to get trampled!"

The last thing she saw was the big brass drum.

Mrs. Stickney wiped the tears of laughter from the corners of her eyes as she set the pages down. "Oh, Joanne. This is a marvelous story. So is the shot Ken got of Russ Vincent going one way while the band went the other."

Simone agreed. The editor sat cross-legged on top of her desk, eating half a tuna sandwich. "It's going to fill that spot on the front page just perfectly. We'll caption the picture: THIS IS LEADERSHIP?"

"That's great," Joanne said, glad the accident had knocked Christina's pyramid photo out of the paper.

"And you really weren't hurt?"

Joanne gave a rueful smile and backed up so she could perch on top of her own desk. "Just my ego. All those band members were walking *around* me, not *over* me."

Simone shook her head again. "You can't buy pictures like that."

"It was just being in the right place at the right time," Joanne added.

The following Saturday night Joanne sat alone in her bedroom. It was the night of the Valentine's Day dance, and she passed the time glancing over the *Trailblazer*s that had featured her fledgling literary efforts. It was appropriate, she thought as she reread her write-up of the competitions. First the parade had marched over her, and now it was marching past her.

Because she had to put so much time into studying, she had no time for her friends, who routinely forgot about her when planning their social activities. All of the boys considered her out of circulation, so no one had asked her to the dance. Actually, she had had one invitation—from Cliff Wright. But there was no point in accepting it because her parents would never have lifted her curfew and grounding. So while other Fremont girls—including Lynn—were getting ready for the dance, Joanne fixed a dinner tray and took it to her room. She ate by the window, watching the stars dust the evening sky. A single tear traced its way down her cheek.

She put her chin on her palm, leaning on the windowsill. "I could do Scarlett O'Hara," she said to herself softly, "and cry that this will never, never happen to me or my family again. I don't want the parade to pass me by. Grounded or not, I'm never going to stay home again." How she would arrange it, she did not know.

Chapter Eight

Two weeks later, Joanne sat staring into her bedroom mirror. "Whoever you're going to be tonight, you had better be good. And charming. And witty." She took a deep breath, put her chin in her hands, and leaned forward. "One thing for sure. Nobody ever likes me for myself."

Her cause for concern was twofold. Earlier in the week Mrs. Stickney had assigned the girls in her journalism class to cover the base-ball game against Fremont's chief rival, Central High. The idea was to get a feminine point of view on the game; the best one would be published in the paper.

Joanne pictured all the wonderful things she'd be able to write about Rob's glowing performance. What a perfect way to win him back, to show him how she could help him. During Spanish class that morning she casually dropped by his desk to tell him she'd be at the game and was thrilled when he agreed to her request for a postgame interview. *Maybe we'll even stop for a bite to eat*, she thought at the time, noting Christina's empty desk.

If she were to go somewhere with Rob, she would first have to do something about Cliff. Ever since the day of the competitions, he'd begun to chat with her regularly in study hall. Joanne was always careful to keep the talks on impersonal topics, but that morning he had surprised her by asking if she wanted to go to the game with him. She was about to tell him no, when she realized how stupid that would look. She was going to the game by herself, a fact Cliff would become painfully aware of as soon as he spotted her. He seemed like a nice enough guy, and she didn't want to hurt him. But she'd have to tread very carefully when Rob was ready to talk to her after the game.

Still in front of her mirror, Joanne mentally ran through the list of personalities she liked to do. Brooke Shields wasn't right, neither was Barbara Walters. Barbra Streisand might carry it off, but then again she was too independent for Rob. Mae West could vamp him, but she would look ridiculous on a high-school baseball diamond. And none of the others came close to fulfilling her needs.

She traced a fingertip around the reflection of her face in the mirror. There wasn't a soul in the world she could do—unless she did herself. "Well, I guess I've got to try it sometime," she said out loud.

Joanne had held onto Rob's acceptance of a postgame interview the way a drowning person holds onto a life preserver. She had convinced herself his "maybe" meant "definitely," and she was preparing for this encounter as if it were a date.

While she was brushing her hair, she heard a gentle rap on the door. "Joanne?"

"Come in, Mom."

Mrs. Palmer came in cautiously. She smiled approvingly at the made bed, then carefully sat down on its corner. "You're spending a lot of time preening for an assignment. You didn't sneak a date in on us, did you?"

Joanne dropped her hairbrush and turned around. "Oh, Mom!"

Her mother's lips tightened. "I thought so." She sighed. "You know that's not part of the agreement."

"It's not a date really. Cliff is just my escort to the game, and he's bringing me right home after it's over. And it is an assignment—I wouldn't be going otherwise." She didn't dare tell her mother about Rob.

"I see, dear." Mrs. Palmer examined the fingernails on her left hand slowly. "Your grades have been picking up, and you're getting your homework done. This once, OK. Next time, we'll talk about it first."

Joanne got up and hugged her mother. "Thanks a lot. Uh—are you going to tell Dad?"

"He's busy with a client this weekend. I don't think it's necessary to bother him, as long as you're home early. Don't stretch your curfew, though."

"All right." Joanne reached for her notebook and purse, then followed her mother out of the room.

Joanne and Cliff were two of the last people to get on the bus. They walked past the cheerleaders, who were standing by their seats in the front of the bus, leading a cheer.

"Lean to the left, lean to the right. Stand up, sit down, fight, fight, *fight!*"

Looking for two adjacent seats, Joanne did not notice Christina glaring at her. Joanne nodded and said hi to several girls who were in her journalism class. Finally she and Cliff sat down toward the rear of the bus, in the seats over the wheel wells.

As soon as Joanne put her purse on the floor, Cliff was nudged by a boy sitting behind him. While Cliff was engaged in a conversation, Joanne turned her attention to his outfit. He was dressed neatly and conservatively in cords, an oxford shirt, and a pullover. Neat, yes—

and boring, she thought. Especially when she thought of Rob and the funky shirts he liked to wear. Joanne wasn't sure why she felt the need to compare the two, but she did, and in the clothing department, at least, Cliff came up wanting.

The bus started up, and the driver shouted, "No standing. All right already, no standing, please." Reluctantly, everyone sat down.

Cliff turned back to Joanne. "Johnny says Central is going to cream us. I bet him he was wrong."

She stared into his eyes for a second before mumbling, "You didn't bet money did you?" Joanne chewed on her thumb. "It's going to be a really tough game tonight," she added worriedly.

Cliff's response was cut off by the sudden arrival of Christina. She had gotten up from her seat in the front and walked back to where Joanne was sitting. She hadn't spoken to Joanne since the competition, and now she towered over her silently, staring at her with icy, blue eyes.

Joanne broke the silence. "Hi, Christina. Your hair looks sensational."

Christina managed a half-smile and then shot back, "I saw you get on the bus, and I just had to find out why you were coming along."

"I didn't know the games were restricted to members of the pep squads," Joanne said tartly. "I thought all of us students were allowed to watch."

"Come on, Joanne, we both know exactly why you're here. And I don't like it."

"I happen to be here for journalism class. It's an assignment."

"You really expect me to believe that?" She snorted. "You better just keep away from Rob, or so help me—"

"Rob's not your property."

"Consider yourself warned," Christina said, fuming. "So you'd better forget all those ideas about him that are floating around in your head." With that she stomped to the front of the bus.

"What a temper!" Cliff, who'd been an unwilling eavesdropper, felt bad for Joanne. "What's she talking about?"

"Oh, nothing," Joanne said. "I'm supposed to interview Rob after the game, and Christina goes crazy whenever he's around another girl."

Cliff started another conversation, leaving Joanne lost in thought. Since Christina hadn't been in Spanish class, Joanne had mistakenly assumed she was sick and wouldn't be going to the game. Now Christina would probably fix it so that Rob wouldn't dare come near her after the game. Joanne would have to think of something. She was ready to fight Christina all the way for Rob's affections; she had to get him away from that witch once and for all.

* * *

At last the bus rolled into the Central High parking lot. The field up ahead was ablaze with lights, and both teams were out doing their warm-up exercises.

Joanne couldn't miss Rob. As team captain, he was organizing drills and assigning people to shag flies. He waved to her as she walked over to the bleachers and took a seat next to Cliff. She watched as Christina sauntered over to him and gave him a hug. He squeezed Christina's hand and moved a curl off her shoulder. Then Christina put her arms around Rob's neck and gave him a long kiss.

The sinking feeling in Joanne's stomach dropped to somewhere around her toes. How could she think she still had a chance with Rob after that public display?

Cliff said, "I'm going to get a drink. Can I get you anything?"

It was all she could do to reply, "Uhh, no, thank you." She watched Christina trot past, her short skirt bouncing, as she joined the rest of the pep squad on the benches in front of the stands. Joanne swallowed and tried to act normally. She waved at blurs she thought were friends. Her hands trembled, so she held them in her lap to quiet them down. In spite of the cool night air, her face felt warm and flushed. Why was she so willing to play the fool whenever Rob was around?

Cliff returned with a Coke just as a recording of the national anthem was being played over the loudspeaker. He nudged Joanne to stand, and as she rose she felt he must think she was some kind of zombie. She tried to think of something funny to say, but her mind was blank. She didn't know what to do about Rob.

The first few innings passed quickly, and Joanne found she was not taking many notes. She stood up and yelled when Cliff did, but at what she didn't know. She could see only Christina prancing around on the edge of the field, waving pom-poms and doing song routines. *Oh, for a poison dart!*

Joanne looked out at the field, trying to concentrate on the game. Fremont was behind, four to two. She saw Rob standing with the coach outside the visitors' dugout, and they appeared to be arguing about something. Rob took his glove out of his back pocket, threw it on the ground, and walked a few steps away in disgust.

Behind her someone said, "Who does that kid think he is, anyway? He's had more arguments tonight than Billy Martin."

She squinted her eyes to see Rob more clearly. An assistant coach caught up with Rob and handed him back his glove. Rob snatched it away and strode quickly back into the shadowed dugout.

When he came up to bat, he struck out in

three furious swings. He brushed past the coach without a word as he returned to the bench.

Partway through the next inning, Cliff said, "I'm really thirsty. Would you mind if I went for another Coke?"

"No, of course not," she answered, more pleasantly than she felt.

"Great. I'll get you one, too." He climbed over the other spectators and disappeared around the end of the bleachers.

When Cliff returned, he handed Joanne a cup. As he squeezed back into his space, he added, "What's happening?"

"More of the same. We're back on the field again." She watched Rob trot to first base. She knew him well enough to know he had a chip on his shoulder. The first batter popped a fly ball toward Rob. He backed up. The right fielder came in.

Cliff jumped to his feet, yelling, "Look out!" His warning was lost in the shouts of others as Rob and the outfielder slammed into each other. The ball bounded away, and the batter ended up safe on third before the commotion ended.

The two Fremont players squared off, arms waving, and Rob threw his glove to the ground again. The umpire came out to separate them. Rob kicked first base savagely before putting his glove back on.

"He's going to get thrown out of the game," Cliff observed as he sat down next to Joanne.

She sighed, realizing there was no way she could ever do a glowing write-up of Rob. Sadly she noted the brawl in her notes.

Central scored two more runs before the game was over. As they stood up to leave, Cliff said, "At least Rob wasn't thrown out. But he sure didn't help us. It's too bad, losing an important game like this."

"Sorry you lost your bet," Joanne said flatly.

There was silence on the returning bus, because everyone was depressed over the loss.

As Joanne and Cliff stood together in the Fremont High parking lot, she decided it was the perfect time to try to make Rob jealous. She just had to let him see her with Cliff. The team bus was just pulling into the lot.

"I really liked sitting at the game with you, Cliff," she said sweetly.

"I liked it, too, Joanne. I'm glad you said yes." He looked down at her, an unreadable expression on his face. Joanne sensed a kind of tension building up inside him and pressed closer. "Shall we go now?" he asked.

"In a minute. I've got to talk to Rob for my article, remember?"

"I don't think he's going to be in a talkative mood."

"I'm the press, he'll talk," she answered.

Cliff walked Joanne to the bus. As soon as Rob got out, Joanne felt her heartbeat increase.

But just as she was about to pounce on him, Christina appeared, seemingly from out of nowhere. Hands clasped, the pair began to walk into the parking lot.

Undaunted, Joanne made her move. With notebook open and pencil ready she called, "Excuse me, Rob. Could I have a few words with you?"

Rob turned around. His hair was slicked down, and bright red spots of anger stained his cheeks.

From the look on his face, Joanne could tell he didn't want to have anything to do with her.

"Say, Joanne, who are you 'doing' tonight?" he asked, sarcasm dripping from his voice.

Cliff, who had walked up behind Joanne, asked, "What's that supposed to mean?"

Rob laughed. "Oh, you know Joanne. She likes to pretend she's other people. She can be real funny when she feels like it."

Joanne's throat tightened. Why was Rob making fun of her? Christina must have had something to do with it.

He leaned toward her, scratching his jaw. "I hope you got some good copy tonight. Sorry, I'm in no mood for an interview."

Cliff put his hand on Joanne's arm, drawing her away. "I think I'll get Jo home early. We both have pretty heavy homework loads with our evening classes."

Rob looked piercingly at her. "How *are* your

night classes? I hear you're getting your senior requirements finished so you can graduate."

"I—I—ah," she stammered, but Cliff interrupted her.

"She's taking accelerated classes, aren't you, Joanne?"

Joanne's throat froze. Not a word came out.

Rob gave a short and cruel laugh. "Advanced classes? Not Joanne!"

"Rob," Joanne said. "Just because you lost the game—"

"Come on, Jo, don't look so shocked."

"Come on," Cliff said in her ear. "I'm taking you home."

Tears stung her eyes. Why did he talk to her like that, in front of everyone? Cliff walked away with her.

What he said in the car, she never really heard. She was in shock and felt numb all over. When Cliff pulled to a stop, Joanne hardly recognized her own house.

The seat creaked as Cliff moved. "I'm sorry about tonight," he said finally. "Sometimes when people hurt, they want everybody to hurt."

"Forget it, it's not your fault."

He hesitated. "Is it true about the evening classes?"

"No! Yes. Oh, shoot . . ." Joanne looked stubbornly out the window. "What do you care?"

"I can't believe it's true, that's all. I do care.

You're intelligent and sweet. Why would you want to pretend with me?"

"It's what I do best," she said lamely.

"What about what he said about your pretending to be other people. Is that true, too?"

"Yes," she admitted.

She looked down so she didn't have to see the hurt expression on Cliff's face. He wasn't supposed to take it so personally—but she could see he had. "So you've been playing games with me. Old Cliff the fool." He shook his head.

"It's not like that," she said.

"And I thought you liked me."

"I do like you, Cliff," she said, trying to make him feel better.

"Maybe you're playing games with yourself, too," he added. "Good night, Joanne." He leaned over and opened her door.

Without saying another word, Joanne bolted out of the car. She raced up the porch steps, threw herself at the door, and frantically turned the knob. Once inside, she was aware that the car did not start for a long time—not until she had stumbled upstairs into her bedroom.

Joanne threw herself on the bed. She never wanted to see Cliff or Rob again!

Chapter Nine

Friday night's disaster kept replaying in Joanne's mind. How could Rob have done such a thing to her? She balanced her chin on her hands as she sat in the journalism classroom the following Wednesday. Love shouldn't hurt, she told herself. It did in movies and songs, but not in real life. Not once had she seen her mother and father deliberately hurt each other.

She doodled on the scratch paper in front of her. As much as she tried, she couldn't focus her mind to work on the assignment of the month. One of the journalism students was going to get a full-page spread for his or her story about Color Day, the day when the students took over Fremont campus. It was the event that signaled the beginning of spring and the senior class madness that was sure to follow.

The assignment was important to her, but she couldn't begin. Most of her stories were written while she pretended to be someone else. But it was becoming more and more difficult for her to "do" anybody.

It looked as if Joanne Palmer would make it, though. Her grades had come up because of a few more good papers in journalism and another decent test grade in history. She was doing well in her night classes, too. She had slipped into a schedule of work and study, but it hadn't been as painful as she had originally imagined. Maybe it was worth it in order to reach certain goals. If she kept it up, she thought she could get her parents to lift her curfew in a few weeks.

The only pain in her life, it seemed, was caused by Rob McAllister. Yet, as cruel as he had been to her the night of the game, she saw him hurting himself more. The boy who had everything was fast losing all that he had, judging by the last game. Baseball meant a lot to Rob. He had already been accepted into a state university on a baseball scholarship, the size of which was to be determined by his performance his last season. She understood why he had gotten so upset at the team's losing. She knew what it was like to lose a dream—after all, he had been hers.

Everyone, she thought, deserves a second chance. If Rob ever talked to her again, she'd be there.

Sighing, Joanne dropped her left hand from her chin and focused on the paper in front of her. The Color Day write-up was one of the hardest things she had ever tried, made harder by her total lack of enthusiasm for the event itself. Color Day was the same old thing every year. All it ever was was a turnover in power at the school for one day. What did it accomplish? So what if students took over the administration? So what if kids taught the classes? What did it prove? The only good thing, Joanne thought, was the Sadie Hawkins dance that followed in the evening.

It was all a joke, she thought. Then inspiration struck, She would write a satire of the whole day. Her pencil began to scratch across the paper. She'd call it the Color Day Revolution. And who better to lead the revolution than Cliff, the last person in the world who'd revolt against anything.

Joanne figured Cliff would be complimented by being the subject of her piece. After she had seen his reaction after the game, she felt bad about trying to use him to make Rob jealous, and, as a result, had avoided him in study hall all that week.

Biting her lip in concentration, Joanne

wrote furiously and almost didn't hear the voice calling from the outer classroom.

"Jo?"

She gasped and bolted upright at the table. Her heart was thumping madly.

"Hey! I didn't mean to scare you." Rob leaned in through the doorway. "I didn't know you were alone." He shifted his books from one hand to the other. "But I'm glad you are."

Joanne swallowed hard. "That's all right," she stammered. She turned her papers face down and swiveled the chair around. "Where's your faithful shadow?"

He winced. "I guess I deserved that."

"Why aren't you in practice?"

He shrugged. "The coach benched me. You really OK? I didn't want to startle you."

"Oh, yeah." But her heart was still racing.

Rob took a deep breath as though his chest hurt. "Ah—listen, Jo. I owe you an apology." He looked up at the ceiling and gave an embarrassed laugh. "We have to stop meeting like this, you know?"

She put her chin in the air. Maybe Katharine Hepburn would make her relax. "Then meet me in the open." *Take charge, demand nothing but the best.*

He put his hand up. "I came looking for you. I kept thinking about the hurt look in your eyes. About Friday night . . . I was under a lot of pressure, and I—I lost my cool. That's hard for me to say, you know. You always believe the best about me."

"I thought you liked that."

"I do. I—uh—I miss it."

"It's OK, Rob. Don't worry about it." *No nonsense. Business conducted; people forgiven. Chin up in the air. Go, Katharine.* Feeling much more at ease, Joanne reached for her pencil, but Rob lingered in the doorway.

"Uh—by the way, who wrote up the baseball game?"

"What?" Joanne looked up, surprised he was still there. She pulled her attention away again. "Ginny Jones. Mrs. Stickney had all the girls write articles. Hers was the best. It's going in tomorrow, be out on Monday."

"I guess it's really a madhouse around here the final day before deadline."

"You bet. What you see now is the calm before the storm." As Joanne watched Rob, she found herself tapping her pencil, à la Hepburn. She stilled it.

"I've got to stop that story. How do I do it?"

"You've got to *what*?"

He waved a hand, and she noticed it was trembling. "I don't know what else to do, Jo! I don't want that story to come out. I'll look really bad."

A chill ran down Joanne's back. She rubbed her arm and stared for a long time at Rob's face. He flinched under her gaze. "I can't help you," she said finally.

"You're right. You don't need to rub it in. I should have thought about it at the game, but I didn't. You know how I am. I jump in with both feet."

"Rob!"

"Listen," he pleaded. "The whole school and the coach already know. I'm not hiding it from anybody here. But that paper goes out all over the state to scouts and other coaches. You know what that can mean to me?"

"It'll mean the whole state will know you had a temper tantrum on the field." Joanne winced inside, but Katharine Hepburn did not.

"That could kill my scholarship!" Rob looked at her. "I'd do anything, Jo, anything to have that story pulled."

"Tell Mrs. Stickney or Simone. I have nothing to do with it."

"There isn't time! I tried to get hold of them. You're the only one here." Pain edged his words. "I'm begging you—please. I can't undo this mess without your help."

She knew she ought to have her head examined for agreeing. "I shouldn't do this for you, Rob. But I will . . . if you'll do something for me."

His expression softened, and his eyes lit up. "Anything, Jo. You name it. You'll never know how much this means to me."

"You owe me more than thanks." She dropped her gaze and couldn't meet his eyes as she said, "I want you to take me to the Sadie Hawkins dance."

"You what? C'mon, Jo, you know about Christina and me."

"Has she asked you yet?"

He shifted awkwardly. "Well, no—"

"Then there's no problem," she said briskly. "You said you'd do anything for me."

"But the dance?" he whined.

Joanne could see he was weakening. "It'd square us. I'd never ask you for anything else again." After the dance, she figured she wouldn't have to.

Rob didn't say a word as he contemplated the proposition. "All right, Joanne," he said finally. "I'd hate to say no to an offer like that."

Joanne smiled triumphantly. "You won't regret it, Rob." Then, as an afterthought, she added, "Oh, um, there's one more thing. I've got a ten o'clock curfew."

"You want me to take you to the dance for an hour?"

"That's all."

Rob shrugged, puzzled. "OK, then." The atmosphere became awkward. "Yeah, well, gotta go." He disappeared so suddenly, she wondered if he had really been there.

Joanne sat very still, thinking of what she had just done. It didn't take much of Hepburn's good old-fashioned Yankee common sense to know that a scholarship and a future were more important than a story in a high school paper. She rationalized that Mrs. Stickney and Simone would agree, too, if they were around. She stood up and wandered over to Simone's desk. The planning sheets lay on top. She had seen the story and knew it was in the top drawer, clipped together with other selected stories.

Hesitantly she opened the drawer. For Rob, she told herself, but she knew it was for Joanne Palmer, too. This was the way she was going to get him back. Nobody was better for Rob than she was. If she had been with him all along, she would never have let him miss practices—and he would never have blown up during that game.

The copy lay on top, right where Joanne knew it would be. Her fingernail snagged on the paper clip as she picked it up. Then she crumpled it up quickly, before she lost her nerve. She would throw it away on the way home. After all, the *Trailblazer* was just a high-school newspaper. Not printing the story could mean a college education for Rob. But why then did she feel like she was betraying her best friend? Joanne took a deep breath and reminded herself she was doing it for Rob. Grabbing her books, she ran from the classroom.

Chapter Ten

The following morning Joanne caught up with Rob after Spanish class.

His face flushed a little—Rob McAllister, blushing!

"Oh, hi," he said. "Uh, how are you today?"

"Just fine. I took care of that matter you asked me about."

His gaze flickered, then grew steady. "All right."

"I threw away the copy."

"I don't want to know how you handled it! Listen, I'm going to be late. See you." He ran off quickly and disappeared down the hall before she could say another word.

At 11:00 A.M. panic erupted in room 103A. Deadline. Joanne couldn't get used to the havoc;

students running here and there; Simone, normally quiet, shouting her head off; Mrs. Stickney thumping on a typewriter in the classroom, urging other typists to hurry, hurry, hurry.

And that was before they discovered Ginny's copy on the baseball game was missing.

Simone kicked her desk drawer shut. "I've looked all over, and it's not here!" she shouted at George Carruthers, the senior sports-page editor. "Are you sure you gave me the story?"

"You know I did, and I have witnesses!" He stood over his drafting table, pasting up copy.

Simone tugged on her braid. Finally she sighed. "Only one thing to do then. Tell Mrs. Stickney."

"Tell me what, Simone?" The journalism teacher asked as she walked into the office. The typists in the other room noticeably slackened speed. Mrs. Stickney made an exasperated sound and then turned back to her editor. "What's wrong?"

"I've lost a sports story. Now I've got all that blank space!"

"What's the story?"

"The baseball game against Central."

"Oh, that? What's the problem? I've got fifteen write-ups of the game, remember?" She walked over to her desk and fumbled through her files. "Here, see if you can use any of these." Simone and George looked at her dumbly, cursing themselves for not having thought of the other articles. "Now what are you waiting for?" Mrs. Stickney asked. "Time's a-wasting!"

Joanne ducked her head down before they caught her staring. She was doomed, and she felt a tightness in her chest that wouldn't go away. Now what could she do?

As it turned out, nothing. But Rob had no reason to complain about the outcome, either. There was so much news that week, the article about the game had to be cut down to only three paragraphs. Rob wasn't mentioned at all, his outburst deemed unnewsworthy by Simone and George.

Nevertheless, after a day or so, it became apparent to Joanne that Rob was avoiding her. She knew how it was done, because she had been avoiding Cliff. Both of them seemed to be getting awfully good at it.

Mrs. Stickney stopped her on the following Thursday as Joanne worked through lunch. "Joanne?" The journalism teacher approached her carrying a sheaf of papers in her hand. "Have you got a minute?"

"Well, yes." Joanne looked longingly in the direction of the PE fields. She had hoped to catch up with Rob and firm up the plans for their date. "Sure, I've got a minute." *Lois Lane can wait another minute or two before searching for Superman.*

"Good." Mrs. Stickney tapped the papers. "I'm announcing it tomorrow, but I wanted to congratulate you in private about your Color Day story. It's unique and witty, and we're going to run it."

"My story?" Joanne couldn't believe she heard properly.

"Yes. I found out it wasn't your idea to take journalism, but I want you to know that I'm pleased with the work you're doing. I think you are, too. There's nothing like seeing your name in print!"

Warm pleasure flushed her. "Really?" she said to herself as Mrs. Stickney walked away.

The wind could not keep up with Joanne as she ran across the open courtyard. It was a day for miracles. She saw Rob moving along the walkway to the boys' locker room—alone. Out of breath, she called to him.

"Rob! Hey, Rob!"

He kept moving.

"Rob, wait up."

He turned slowly. He looked coldly down at her as she ran up.

"Didn't you hear me calling?"

"I think the whole school heard you. What do you want?"

His attitude flustered her. "My Color Day story—well, ah—" She stopped. His coldness sucked the pleasure right out of her.

"Listen, I'm in a big hurry. We'll talk some other time." He started to swing around.

He was obviously in one of his crabby moods. "Are you playing again?" she asked instead.

It was obvious she had struck a raw nerve. "Yes, I'm playing. And, no, I'm no longer the team captain." He flicked his watch up so she could see it. "We're both late, OK? I'm leaving."

"Rob!" she called in surprise as he lumbered off. "I'm sorry about—" The back of his windbreaker rippled in the breeze as he walked away. She hugged her notebook to herself. "It was nothing important, anyway," she finished lamely. In a small voice nobody heard, she added, "I just got the whole front page under my by-line for Color Day." The second buzzer sounded, jerking her back. "Oh, no!" She ducked her head and ran to her history class.

"Doesn't this look nice." The journalism teacher held up the Color-Day issue of the *Trailblazer*. Turning to Joanne, she smiled. "Well, young lady, you certainly have made a splash."

Joanne laughed at the old-fashioned term. Her smile stayed, however, as she looked at the paper. Her feature, Color Day Revolution, ran column to column. The masthead had been done specially in colored ink (blue and gold, of course) for the story.

Pride filled her for a moment. It almost made up for how rotten she felt about throwing away the baseball article. Even though it turned out not to have made a difference, she couldn't shake the guilt of her act, and she knew that someday she would have to tell Mrs. Stickney and Simone the truth. No one had suffered from it but her. Rob had promised to be grateful—but the harder she tried with him, the more distance he put between them. She couldn't figure out why, though she was sure Christina was at the center of it.

Simone looked at Joanne speculatively. "Don't you wish you'd been on the paper sooner? You could have been a page editor, too."

"And have your worries? I like it just the way it is. Besides, this is fun for me. I just sort of play around with it. I'm not worried about making it a career or anything."

"Well, your work is terrific. I like a humorous approach to life." She tapped the stack of papers in front of her. "Ken, this one is ready."

Nodding, Ken bent over and picked the stack up, lugging it out of the door. Two sophomores trotted out after him with bundles of their own.

Simone dusted her hands symbolically. "As my dad would say, 'Another day, another dollar.' That's it for a week and a half. Then deadline, and we start all over." She slipped her braid over her shoulder. "Going to the Sadie Hawkins dance, Jo?"

"Yeah, but I'm still pretty much on curfew."

"After all your good grades?" Mrs. Stickney asked in surprise.

"Yeah, well, I've got a lot to make up for."

"Your parents were pleased, though, weren't they?"

"Sure were. Especially my dad. He said he'd given up on me." Joanne scratched the tip of her nose and said in a deep voice, "Jo, baby, I didn't know you had it in you. Well, carry on, carry on."

Simone laughed. "Joanne! Your father doesn't sound like that!"

"Oh, no? He's an accountant, isn't he? Dull, dull, dull."

"Nobody dull could have sired a spitfire like you," the silver-haired teacher told her, smiling. "Now, come on. It's lunchtime. Get yourselves out of here."

As Simone and Joanne hurried out, the tall girl adjusted her long steps to Joanne's shorter ones. She pushed a paper into her hand. "Show Lynn this. I'll see you later," and she hurried off to meet her boyfriend, who was coming out of the tower.

In the cafeteria, Lynn trotted up to Joanne with steaming hamburgers in both hands and a package of freshly baked cookies in her teeth. Her eyes widened as Joanne flashed the paper in front of her. They wove their way through the crowded tables to an empty spot.

"Joanne! You didn't tell me it was going to look so sensational!" Lynn said as she dropped the cookies on the tabletop. She swung her legs over and settled on the bench, snatching the paper from Joanne's hands.

Joanne spread her hands in mock apology. "I didn't know, either. You never know for sure what the paper's going to look like. You get all the pieces right, but the whole picture is never there until the very end." She unwrapped her burger, adding. "I'm glad you like it. I know how much you hate getting my lunch and all."

"For this it's worth it."

"Um—one other thing. I forgot my lunch money. Pay you tomorrow?"

"I'll take a pound of flesh." There was silence while she devoured a cookie. "On the other hand, you don't have too much to spare these days. Maybe I'll just take your money."

Joanne smiled, pleased that her friend could tell she was getting thinner. All that running around the campus really had made a difference; she had lost nearly ten pounds since Christmas.

Lynn pulled the paper close, reading while she ate. Her face grew solemn as she read on, and Joanne grew curious. She tapped the page.

"Jo, did anybody read this first?"

"Sure. Mrs. Stickney and Simone both. Why?"

"Oh, nothing. But—maybe—don't you think you're kind of hard on Cliff?"

"Hard, no! It's a satire. It's meant to be funny. What are you talking about?" Joanne crumpled up the bag her hamburger had come in and tried to grab the *Trailblazer*, but Lynn wouldn't let go of it. "Doonesbury couldn't have done a better job."

"Yeah, but not everybody appreciates being roasted in *Doonesbury*. If you had written this about me, I—" Lynn hesitated.

"You what?"

"I just wouldn't like it." Lynn shoved the paper away suddenly. "I'd hate to think you did this just for a story. But then, I'm not like everybody else."

"You sure aren't!" Joanne folded the paper up. She had to change the subject fast. "So what are you wearing to the dance?"

"Oh, I haven't decided. Probably jeans."

Joanne nodded. "I think that's what I'll probably wear, too."

Lynn nearly swallowed her retainer. "You're going?"

Joanne had wanted to surprise Lynn by showing up at the dance with Rob, but she couldn't hold in the secret any longer. "I'm going with Rob."

"You must be kidding! After what he's put you through? You really are a glutton for punishment."

"You can't give up on what you really want," Joanne said seriously. "You just don't understand real love."

"I don't think you do, either. I think you want him because you can't have him. You never seemed to be this crazy about him when you were dating. You always told me he was too macho."

"Yeah, but those kisses."

Lynn nibbled her last bit of cookie. "Your parents are letting you go?"

"Yeah, but I can't stay after ten o'clock."

Lynn shook her head in disbelief. "You're kidding? You're going to go for an hour?"

"Half a loaf is better than none."

"I can't stand it when you get philosophical. How'd you get him to go with you, anyway? Christina's still got him wrapped around her little finger."

"I was hoping she was out of it. I haven't seen her draped around him lately."

"His dad made him drop her for two weeks, until he was made captain again. But they've been burning up the telephone wires."

"Says who?"

"Says Cathy Turner. And back to the other questions—how'd you get him?"

Joanne shook her head. "Not telling." Out of the corner of her eye, she saw Cliff Wright looking over the lunch tables. She hoped he liked her article. Even so, she had no desire to confront him yet.

Nevertheless, he caught her eye, as if she had been the person he was looking for. As he came over, his rangy, self-assured gait looked unusually subdued. He held a crumpled-up *Blazer* in his hand.

"Hi, Cliff," Lynn mumbled.

He didn't notice her. "I saw the paper, Joanne," he said evenly.

"Did you like the story? It was the best Doonesbury I could come up with."

He looked hurt, just like a little boy who'd had a door shut in his face.

"I thought we were friends. Of all the people at school, you should know more than anyone else how I feel about the job I was elected to. I'd never do anything crazy like lead a revolt against the school. I know I'm kind of straight, but I don't think I deserve anything as terrible as this. What did I ever do to you?"

Her cheeks flamed. "Where's your sense of humor, Cliff? It's supposed to be a joke. Something silly—just like Color Day itself."

"It's not funny when you're the pincushion instead of the pin." He threw the wadded-up paper on the table and walked away.

"Cliff?" Joanne called after him, puzzled. "Cliff?" But he was gone, and the bell rang, ending lunch period.

Lynn brushed past her, remarking. "I guess I'm not the only weird person in town."

Joanne grabbed her books off the table. "Some people have no sense of humor."

"And some people have no sensitivity."

"What do you mean by that?"

"I mean if you hadn't been so busy 'doing' Doonesbury, you might have seen the real Cliff. You would have known he'd take it personally."

"I didn't mean to hurt him. You've got to believe that."

"Don't tell me. Go tell him, if you can catch up with him. You know, Jo, you've had a great time writing for the paper, but you've used people to get your stories. Paul, Cliff—and even Rob a little. I like 'doing' people; I think it's funny. But when they start to run you instead of other way around . . . I don't know. Maybe it's time you read what you've been writing."

"Come on, Lynn!" Joanne looked at her friend, shocked by what she was saying. "That's not true, and you know it!"

"I hope you're right. But I still think you owe him an apology."

As the warning buzzer sounded, Joanne ran off to climb the tower to Broadhurst's class, her stomach knotted in confusion. So far she hadn't done anything right! Helping to keep Rob's name out of print hadn't brought him back, and putting Cliff's name in print had driven him away. Barbara Walters, Katharine Hepburn, Doonesbury, and the rest of them certainly had gotten her in a huge mess. Who, she wondered, was going to get her out of it?

Chapter Eleven

Lynn became consumed with curiosity about Joanne's pending date with Rob. Joanne refused to go into any of the details as to how she had gotten him to agree, only assuring her friend that by the time Rob took her home from the dance he'd be hers again for good.

Joanne tried to find Cliff to apologize, but he avoided her, staying away from study hall for most of the week. He finally showed up on Thursday, and Joanne approached him cautiously as soon as he took his seat.

She cleared her throat twice before he looked up. "Hey, Cliff, I haven't seen you around here lately."

To her surprise Cliff smiled at her. "I've been busy with a student government project."

"Cliff, I'm really sorry about the article. If I'd known it was going to hurt you like that, I never would have written it."

"Sit down, Joanne. There's something I've got to tell you." Joanne did as he said. "Apology accepted—though you have nothing to apologize for. I'm the one who owes you an apology. Will you accept it?"

"What are you talking about?"

"I shouldn't have blown up at you. See, according to my mom, I've been suffering from a near-fatal case of loss-of-sense-of-humor. When I first saw the article, all I could think of was how it would look to the colleges I'd applied to. But when I told that to my mom, she really got on my case. She thought your article was great—and that I was acting pompous. She made me reread your article. And you know what? It is funny. Now that I think about it, I'm really looking forward to tomorrow's 'revolution.'"

Joanne sighed with relief. "Oh, I'm so glad you feel that way, Cliff. You don't know how upset I've been."

Cliff's face showed his concern. "I should have told you earlier. I just assumed you didn't care."

"Oh, no," Joanne said, looking directly at him. She did care, she'd come to realize that. "I do like you," she said.

"Funny. That's what my mom said. She

told me people often satirize things or people they truly admire."

Joanne felt her face flush. Who could she hide behind now?

"By the way, Jo. Are you going to the dance tomorrow night?"

Why did he have to ask her that? She knew he'd be disappointed with her answer. "Yes," she said softly. "I'm going with Rob McAllister."

Cliff couldn't hide his grimace. "Oh."

"Will you be there?"

"Could the student body president not show up?" he asked, recovering his usual smile.

"Good. I hope to see you there," Joanne said, rising. "Gotta get back to the books," she added, moving back to her desk.

Mrs. Palmer stood in the corner of the kitchen, balancing first on one foot and then the other as she backed up evaluating her watercolor. She turned her attention to Joanne, who had come in to get a glass of water while waiting nervously for Rob. "Hi, dear." She waved at the easel. "How do you like it?"

Joanne tilted her head. "OK, I guess. It is right side up, isn't it?" She ducked as her mother playfully threw a hand towel at her.

"You look nice. Aren't those the jeans your father told you never to wear again—the ones that looked like they were painted on?"

"Yeah." Joanne twirled slowly. "Ten pounds makes a big difference, doesn't it?"

"You look lovely," her mother said, as she sat down again in front of the easel; she twisted in her chair to continue talking to Joanne. "Is it worth it even if you have to be in by ten?"

"Oh, yes!" Joanne grinned again, reflecting the happiness and excitement she felt.

"I bet Rob's other girlfriend—what's her name?—is green because you're going."

"Christina—and yes, she probably is." Joanne was always a little uncomfortable when her mother tried playing best friend with her. Still, she appreciated her mother's support.

The doorbell rang, and Joanne grabbed her jacket, shouting, "Gotta dance!"

"Remember Cinderella," her mother called after her.

"I'll remember." She ran to the front door before Paul could get to it and jerked the door open.

"Hi, Jo," Rob said, flashing a smile.

Her heart went pit-a-pat—or something close to that. Someday she vowed to hold a tape recorder to her chest to see if she could tape the sound. "Hi, Rob. I'm all ready."

"Great."

"Let's go." She stepped outside, and he followed her to the car at the curb. It was his dad's car. Joanne had fond memories of her first kiss from Rob in the front seat of it.

Joanne stood for a moment on the curb, then got in quickly when she realized Rob wasn't going to open the door for her.

Rob was quiet as he drove to the school, which was on the other side of town. After pulling into the parking lot, he turned off the ignition and sat looking at the dashboard for a long time. Finally he said, "C'mon, let's go," and slid out of the car. He strode toward the Fremont gym without looking behind.

Joanne scrambled to get out of the car, and she just caught up with him before he reached the door. Rob continued to walk down the hallway, oblivious to Joanne, who had to trot to keep up. Just as he was about to round a corner, she decided to find out what was happening. "I'm not the quickest study in the world, but something's wrong. What's bugging you?"

Rob leaned against the wall and shrugged. "You, I guess. I'm not going to spend any time with you tonight, Jo. Christina's waiting for me inside. You manipulated me into this, and I don't like it."

His words hurt Joanne badly, and she drew back against the opposite wall. It wasn't supposed to be like this! "It's only for an hour, Rob! And you agreed. For old times' sake."

"For old times' sake! Jo, that's just the point. Sure we had some good times, but they're in the past. They don't exist anymore and haven't in quite awhile. Christina was right. Sometimes you're more like a little puppy dog than a person. Why is it so important for you to be seen with me, anyway?"

"Why is it so important for you to be with Christina?"

"She's an attention-getter, and I like her. She's somebody, Jo."

"And I'm not?"

He chose his words carefully. "You're a lot of fun. You've always been popular. In fact, dating you helped make *me* more popular. But I have different goals now. I'm college-bound and where I go depends on how well I do and who I know."

"And it helps to be seen with Christina."

"Yeah. I nearly blew it last month at that game. I'm only here because you really stuck your neck out for me and tried to bail me out. But I want you to get this and get it straight. I won't ever let you corner me like this again. I know what I want."

"Rob—"

"Don't Rob me. And don't give me that wide-eyed, hurt look. It won't work."

"All right, Rob," she said slowly. "I guess I deserve this." She stopped as her voice quavered.

His eyes softened. "I'm sorry, Joanne. Look, I know there are plenty of guys in there who are dying to dance with you."

"Forget it."

120

"No, I mean it. Now, I've got to go. Christina's waiting."

"Someday, when you realize who's really good for you, you'll come back to me."

"Let me go, Joanne."

Then he was gone, off to join Christina at the dance. For a long time Joanne stood where he had left her. Still shaken from the scene, she felt too embarrassed to show her face at the dance. So she wandered aimlessly through the deserted halls, stopping to stare blankly at the bulletin boards of safety hints put up by the Health Club.

Joanne had struck out in a big way, and she wondered just where she had gone wrong as far as Rob was concerned. In all her years of dating, no boy had ever stood her up before. One voice inside her kept telling her that he was the one at fault, that he was simply an uncaring person with whom she should never have become involved. *Let him go*, another, more logical voice said. After a while logic won out, as Joanne made a mental list of Rob's good and bad points. There was no contest, she concluded, he really wasn't worth it. He never really was.

Soon after she had come to this conclusion, she looked up at a wall clock and jumped. It was nine-thirty, and she had no way of getting home!

Instinctively Joanne searched her jeans for

the dime her mother always made her carry. But she found nothing but lint and loose threads. How was she going to call home?

With a flash of inspiration, she ran to the pay phones near the school entrance. Sometimes dimes could be found in the coin returns, she reasoned. But as luck would have it, she found nothing.

Joanne leaned dejectedly against the glass booth. "Well, Stan, that's another fine mess you got us into," she said in her best Oliver Hardy imitation. She pressed her face against the cool surface and sighed. "What am I going to do?" Her only hope was to beg a dime from someone at the dance, but she'd rather take her chances walking home through the dark streets than face that crowd.

"Joanne, is that you?"

She screeched and jumped up a foot. The tall figure hovering over her put up both hands in surrender. Grinning easily, the boy added, "I guess I ought to quit coming at you out of dark corners." Cliff Wright dropped his hands. "C'mon, you look kind of desperate. What are you doing here?"

"Oh, Cliff!" She swallowed her heart and hoped it would end up near the general vicinity it belonged. "Rob kind of left me here. We had a—well, kind of argument."

"I knew something was wrong when I didn't see you with him in there."

"Have you got a dime?"

He fished in his cords for a moment, then handed her a dime.

"You're a lifesaver!" She put the coin in the phone and began to dial. "I've got a ten o'clock curfew, and my mother's going to kill me!"

He took the receiver gently from her hand. "Maybe you'd better let me talk to her." He squeezed into the booth beside her. "Hello, Mrs. Palmer? Hi, this is Cliff Wright. Fine, thanks. Mrs. Palmer, Joanne's had a slight problem at the dance, and I'm coming to her rescue. No, she's fine." He checked his watch. "Well, it's going to take me awhile to get her home. And frankly, if you don't mind, I know my mother's curious to meet her—after the article she wrote and all. Can I bring her back in about an hour or so? OK, I'll have Joanne call from my house. No, nothing's wrong." He looked down at Joanne, the gentle lines of his smile crinkling the corners of his mouth. "No, I think she'd better explain it to you herself. Right. Thanks a lot." He hung up firmly. "Now, you're coming with me."

He took her elbow and steered her out to his car in the parking lot.

"Why are you doing this?" Joanne asked as she sat down and buckled herself in.

"Let's just say you're rescuing me as much as I'm rescuing you."

"Thanks," she said, not knowing exactly what he meant.

"Your mom says it's all right if I could bring you over to my house before I take you home. OK?"

"OK, but my mom *really* said she didn't mind? And what did you mean about my rescuing you?"

Cliff sighed, looking straight ahead as he started the car and drove out of the parking lot. "You know I've liked you ever since I met you in that journalism class. You've always seemed a bit distant with me, but I still got the feeling you liked me, too. I was kind of hoping you'd ask me to the dance, so I turned down every girl who asked me. Then you wrote that article, and I was ready to reconsider—but it was too late. I ended up without a date. I thought I should show up, though, you know, being student-body president and all, but I felt pretty awkward. So, you rescued me, too."

Even though it was dark, Joanne could have sworn she saw a blush creeping up Cliff's face. So quickly she told him the whole story of her ill-fated quest for Rob, including how she had used Cliff. "What's that old saying about not being able to see the forest for the trees?" she concluded. "You were there all this time—and I just didn't see you!"

"I probably shouldn't say this, but you're better off without him."

"I know that now. I just feel stupid for having taken so long to see through him."

"We all make mistakes," he said as he pulled into his driveway.

Cliff's home was a neat, one-story house not far from Joanne's. After he turned off the engine, he opened her door and gave her his hand. She hesitated slightly before taking it.

"Are you sure this is OK?"

"I'm sure. My mom will be delighted. Besides, she's the original lemonade-and-cookies lady. She'll even put a Band-Aid on your ego if you need it. C'mon."

A petite redhead opened the door just as Cliff reached for his keys. "Cliff!" The woman smiled as she saw Joanne standing there. Wearing a paint smock and rolled-up jeans, Cliff's mother looked more like his sister, Joanne thought.

He kissed her on the top of her head. "Hi, Shorty. This is Joanne. Joanne, meet my mother."

Mrs. Wright extended a paint-smeared hand. "Finally! I keep asking Cliff to bring a girl home!" She shot him a playful look.

He grinned and directed Joanne toward the kitchen, from which a warm and familiar smell wafted.

"Cookies?"

"Of course!" Mrs. Wright answered. "It's the

only way to keep him in line. Through his stomach!"

As Joanne trailed in after Cliff, Mrs. Wright asked, "How was the dance? You're back pretty early."

Cliff answered quickly. "Fine. I've got to run Joanne home soon, but I thought she could use some of your provisions first."

"Milk or hot chocolate?" Cliff's mother paused with one finger to her lips as though testing the wind, then decided. "Yes, hot chocolate. The nights are still pretty cool." She patted a chair for Joanne. "The phone's in the corner if you want to call home. Sit down for a few minutes with us if you can. Cliff's all the company I have, and he drives me crazy."

By the time Joanne got off the phone, Mrs. Wright had made a change in the hot-drinks selection. A teapot covered with a hand-quilted cozy sat on the table.

"It goes better with the cookies, don't you agree?" Mrs. Wright said of the tea.

Joanne nodded and relaxed over the fresh lemon cookies and hot spiced tea. "These cookies are fantastic," she said.

Mrs. Wright watched her over the rim of her earthenware teacup. "So this is the lady with the wicked typewriter."

Joanne blushed.

"Mom!" A red-faced Cliff looked into his teacup.

Lydia Wright smiled. "Now, don't get sensitive on me, Cliff. I was complimenting her." She eyed Joanne closely. "You have the wonderful ablity to view the whimsy in everyday things. I've read and enjoyed every one of your stories."

"Thank you. I'm not really—"

"Now don't go putting yourself down. You have a flair for writing. That's a rare gift. Perhaps you need to learn a slightly softer touch, but it's a rare gift nevertheless."

Joanne dunked her last cookie and gobbled it up before it could fall as a soggy mess through her fingers. "Thanks."

"Cliff has told me you go to night school. Accelerated classes, too?"

She hesitated. "Make-up classes to help finish up my credits. Nothing accelerated about that."

"I see." Lydia absentmindedly pushed the cookie plate over in front of Cliff. Then she asked, "How do you like the classes? Are you going on to college?"

"Oh, well, they're OK. It's strictly make-up, for the diploma and graduation. My dad wants me to go on to junior college, though I'm still not sure about that."

"I see." Mrs. Wright smiled, a smile just as open as Cliff's. "What was the trouble tonight?"

She shrugged. "Oh, I had a date with someone who really didn't want to take me out. So he dumped me."

Lydia put a hand on her arm. "I think you've got it handled."

Joanne found herself nodding. She relaxed then as they spent the better part of the next hour telling jokes and laughing a lot. She found it hard to remember that a few hours before, her night had been a total disaster.

When Cliff drove her home, he took the long way around and ended up on Skyline Drive, the hilly street that surrounded their neighborhood. When she saw where he was taking her, Joanne sat up, a smile on her face that was hidden in the darkness. She had been up on Skyline Drive with Rob, but she hadn't expected Cliff to take her.

He stopped the car at the hill's highest point and slipped his seat back slightly. "Pretty up here, isn't it?"

"Yes. I'll bet there's a Skyline Drive in every city in the United States."

It struck him funny, for he started laughing. She joined in.

"I mean, wherever there are teenagers, there's a Skyline-type Drive somewhere. Don't you think?"

He agreed. His hand caressed the back of her neck. Her skin tingled, and she felt goose-bumps all the way down to her toes. But he made no further move, and she sensed he felt a little awkward.

She leaned toward him, tilted her head up, and looked into his eyes. "I think the rescuer deserves a reward." She kissed him quickly, but before she could pull away, he grasped her shoulders and kissed her again, hard. When he let her go, Joanne sat back, shaken.

He started the car quickly. "I think I'd better get you home."

When he walked her to the door, she didn't really want to say goodbye. She stood on the top porch step, her head nearly even with his jaw. "Thanks, I needed that," said Joanne.

"Thought you might. Believe it or not, we all get left flat once in a while."

"I hope that wasn't just a mercy kiss."

He smiled. "No. I was a little selfish about that. I wanted it for myself."

Impulsively she leaned forward and planted a small kiss on his cheek. "Thanks again." She hurried inside, grinning at his bemused expression.

She could learn to like Cliff Wright a lot, she thought dreamily as she prepared for bed. For the first time in months, she wasn't thinking about Rob as she snuggled under the covers.

Chapter Twelve

Lynn clutched Joanne's hand the following Thursday afternoon at the Little Theater. It was white-knuckle time—she was trying out for the senior-class musical. "How do I look?" she asked.

"The truth? You look scared. Pure, unadulterated fear." Joanne added, in case Lynn misunderstood her, "F-E-A-R."

"Don't tell me that! That's all I needed to hear." Then, as if realizing that it was the wrong thing to say, she added, "Oh, I'm really glad you're here."

Joanne peered into the dark recesses of the theater. Mr. Musselman was nowhere to be seen, but there were several students on the stage sitting around reading. She sighed. "Think nothing of it. I just have to be back home by five, or Mom will kill me."

Lynn rolled and unrolled her copies of the script and score.

Joanne grabbed them. "Is that any way to treat *Oklahoma*!?"

Her friend swallowed. "I hate auditions. Not that I've had that many, but still. . . ."

"Look," Joanne said. "Do you want your parents to waste all the money they've put into your braces and dancing and voice lessons? Get up there and break a leg."

"Thanks." Her friend took her retainer out, tucked it into a tissue, and slipped the wad inside her purse. "I don't see Mr. Musselman anywhere, and I'm too nervous to go on stage yet. Why don't we sit down, and you can practice with me for a while, OK?"

"Sure," she agreed. She pulled Lynn down to the third row to sit. Lynn dropped the script in Joanne's lap.

"You play all the other parts as I read Laurey." She stopped and looked quickly at Joanne. "You know, you'd be a terrific Ado Annie."

"Who?"

"You know—the girl who can't say no to anybody."

Joanne raised her eyebrows as she unrolled the script. "That sounds like something I'm good at." She could barely read the words in the dim light.

Lynn read the lead part, Laurey. She stumbled at first, then warmed up. Suddenly she went pale. "I'm gonna be sick!" she cried, before getting up and rushing out.

When Lynn came back into the theater, she walked up to the wall and laid her forehead against its cooling surface. "I'll never make it."

"Aw, come on. Sure you will. All the stars talk about butterflies before they perform."

"Oh, yeah? Name one."

"Miss Piggy." She grabbed Lynn's elbow and towed her toward the stage. "Let's go, trouper."

Mr. Musselman was onstage now, directing. He didn't turn around. But the two of them were approached by one of his assistants.

"Who are you reading for?" the skinny, pale-faced girl asked.

Lynn told her.

"Can you sing and dance?"

"My mother thinks so," answered Lynn, smiling weakly.

The girl marked down a number on a white card and pinned it to Lynn's blouse.

"Number seven, my lucky number," Lynn exclaimed. She patted it for extra luck.

"And you?"

"Oh, I'm just here holding Lynn's hand," Joanne told her. The student nodded and started to turn away.

"That you, Joanne Palmer?" Mr. Musselman asked. He looked down on them from the halo of the stage lights.

"Yes, sir." Joanne was a little surprised as he remembered her.

"She's reading for Ado Annie," Musselman informed his student assistant. She hesitated for a second before marking a large number four on a green card and pinning it to Joanne's sleeve.

"Honestly, Mr. Musselman, I'm not reading for anybody."

"Don't give me that, young lady." The drama teacher wagged a finger at her. "If you have the nerve to rehearse behind my head, you have the nerve to get up on this stage and read for a part. I want you up here."

Confused, Joanne couldn't figure out a way to refuse gracefully. She climbed up on the stage as a drama student stuffed an extra script and score into her hand.

"Nice timing, Joanne," someone said icily.

Joanne whirled around and looked into Christina's cold blue eyes. A green placard bearing the number one was hanging from the songleader's sleeve.

Joanne's arm dropped.

"I thought you got Rob's message."

"This has nothing to do with Rob."

"Oh, no? Don't tell me you didn't know he's auditioning for the lead, Curly. You're still tag-

134

ging after him, huh." Christina's fingertips traced around the outside of her script. "Ado Annie's quite a part," she continued smoothly. "I'm auditioning for her, too."

Joanne closed her mouth firmly, realizing it was senseless to talk to her. She straightened up and walked away to the side of the stage. It was funny, she thought, she hadn't even thought of Rob since the dance, and here was Christina still jealously guarding her turf. But there was something nagging at Joanne. Why should Christina get all the plums in life? Joanne sat on a folding chair and began to read the part of Ado Annie. The singing didn't look too hard.

"It's made for a comedienne with a limited vocal range," Lynn pointed out to her. "You can almost talk your way through it."

The numbers on their cards indicated the order in which they would audition. Joanne first watched Christina and then two other seniors wiggle through the sample number before Mr. Musselman pointed at her.

Lynn slapped her on the shoulder. "It's your turn to break a leg," she whispered.

Holding the score open, Joanne stepped nervously to the front of the stage. Musselman was in the audience, in the third row, slouched down so far in his seat that she'd never have known he was there if the light hadn't bounced off his bald head.

As she was getting ready to begin, the back

door to the Little Theater popped open. The sudden gleam of white light from outdoors was like a spotlight. She couldn't see the face of the figure striding down the aisle, but she knew the walk.

Rob McAllister, come to see his girlfriend perform. But he was too late—in more ways than one.

Christina, who was sitting in the front row, had turned when the door had opened. She had obviously been expecting him, Joanne thought. Christina motioned to Rob, and he came down the aisle and sat beside her. She took his arm possessively, then looked at Joanne. The songleader was obviously intending to throw darts at Joanne while she auditioned. Joanne cleared her throat and took a deep breath.

Why should Christina get all the plums? Joanne toed the mark and stared at her feet. She could do Liza Minnelli, or she could do herself. If ever a part was made for Joanne Palmer . . .

When the piano started, she began to sing "I Cain't Say No." She thought of all the people to whom both she and Ado Annie couldn't say no. Rob and his request to kill the baseball article. Paul and his incessant bratty demands for money. Simone and her assignments. When she finished, perspiration was running down her face. She didn't know how she had fared, but she felt wonderful.

Musselman said nothing, waved her aside, and called for the next actress.

With an embarrassed clearing of her throat, Joanne moved offstage. The natural high ebbed away slowly.

Lynn squeezed her hand. "A little flat, but you'll do."

"What do you think Mr. Musselman thought?"

Her friend shrugged. "What do you care?" she said, teasing.

Joanne didn't answer. But to her surprise, she *did* care, she cared intensely. "I've been acting forever," she told Lynn. "It's about time I got some credit for it."

Finally the auditions for Laurey began. Lynn quavered her way through her song, barely on key, her throat paralyzed with fear. Mr. Musselman gave a slight shake of his head as he made notes, and Joanne prayed Lynn hadn't seen him do it.

Lynn hadn't. She stood glassy-eyed facing the audience until another auditioner edged her away. Then she walked down the steps and over to where Joanne was sitting. She collapsed onto Joanne's arm. "Did I do it? Did I get through it?"

"Don't you remember?"

"My mind's a total blank! I don't remember anything!" Lynn clutched her temples dramatically. "Where am I?"

"You did it," Joanne insisted. She pushed her friend down in the seat beside her. "Now shut up."

The next morning a crowd of seniors was gathered around the bulletin board outside the Little Theater reading the cast list. Joanne was in the back of the group, waiting for Lynn to snake her way to the front. Joanne heard Dana Williams, a pert blond, shout for joy, which was quickly followed by the appearance of Lynn.

"Did you get it?" Joanne asked.

"Dana did—couldn't you hear her?" Lynn said, smiling broadly.

"So why are you so happy?"

"I'm so relieved. Who wants to go through life that petrified? Musselman cast me in one of the extra parts. That's good enough for me—and my parents, I hope. But that's not the only reason I'm smiling. Guess who got Ado Annie?"

Joanne grew white. "Me?" she whispered, her throat tightening in shock.

"You bet. Congratulations, kid."

"Oh." Joanne bit her lip.

"You don't sound too thrilled."

"I'm in shock," she said. "I don't even think my parents will let me get off curfew for this."

"They've got to," Lynn assured her.

"Well, Joanne, what did you really do to get that part?" Christina asked as she approached with Rob. "You know, I've just had it with you," she added, spitting the words out.

Joanne said, "There is such a thing as being a good loser."

"If you won fairly, I'd lose graciously." She looked Joanne up and down.

"But Musselman chose me," she answered.

"Jo, if you think you're going to get me back by doing this, you're dead wrong," Rob put in.

Joanne spat out firmly, "I had no idea you wanted to play Ado Annie, Christina. I auditioned for the role for myself. I didn't try out just to take a part away from you." She surprised herself with the strength of her words.

Rob answered for Christina. "You haven't won yet."

"Rob!" But he turned away, forcing Christina to move with him. Joanne looked after them as Lynn jostled her elbow.

"Way to go, kid. Eat 'em alive. I didn't know you were a tigress inside. Who were you doing that time?"

"Me," Joanne answered, watching them disappear. She sighed, feeling drained. "I thought, Lynn, that we could at least end up as friends someday."

"We are!" Lynn exclaimed, shocked.

"No, no. Not you and me. Me and Rob."

Her friend shrugged and began to walk

139

toward the lockers. "Well, dearie, we showed 'em."

"Yeah, but now what? I've got a part in a play my parents probably won't let me do. The senior barbecue is coming up, not to mention grad night at Disneyland, and the prom." She ticked them off on her fingers. "I'm still on curfew, and I'm going to miss them all."

Lynn looked at her searchingly. "And whom did you expect to be escorting you to all these events? Not Rob!"

Joanne waved at her in disgust. "I never want to see that creep again. But I'm serious, I want the last two months of my senior year to be fun. My mom and dad can't deny me that, can they?"

"I see you still haven't answered my question," Lynn said.

Joanne smiled. "You'll see soon enough," she answered.

Cliff had to miss study hall for some student government business, but he caught up with Joanne at lunch. "Well, congratulations are in order, I see."

"Thanks, Cliff," Joanne said. "I guess it must be all over school by now."

"The play is a pretty important event. I didn't know you were interested in drama."

Joanne laughed to herself, thinking of all the people she'd "done" over the years. "I'm the original role player. Take that article I wrote about you. That wasn't me who wrote it, that was me pretending to be Doonesbury. Hey, I just found out Mrs. Stickney nominated that piece for a countywide journalism competition."

"That's terrific!" Cliff beamed.

"Yeah, and the awards are being presented this Sunday at the junior college. Mrs. Stickney's not one to give a girl much notice. It's exciting, though, isn't it?"

"Hmm. Let me ask you something, Joanne. Since I'm the subject of that article I feel I have a vested interest in seeing how this competition turns out—"

Joanne cut him off. "I have an idea. Why don't you take me?"

"Just tell me the time, and I'll be there," Cliff said.

Joanne smiled. Maybe with Cliff she could have a terrific finish to her senior year after all.

Chapter Thirteen

Sunday afternoon Joanne stood at the curb, waiting for Cliff to take her to the journalism competition. As the familiar tan car pulled up, Cliff leaned over and called out the window, "Hop in."

Joanne sat down, but she didn't bother to shut the car door.

Cliff looked bewildered. "What's the matter? You don't seem too excited."

"You wouldn't be either if this was your only social event for the year."

"Thanks," he grumbled.

"Don't take it personally, Cliff. I don't mean being with you. I mean that Dad still has me on restriction. He won't let me be in the play."

"Why not?"

"Seems my midterms from night school finally came on Friday. I got a B-plus and a B-minus."

"That's great," Cliff interrupted.

"No, it isn't. They were *too* good. Dad figures I did so well *because* I'm on curfew. He said it'd be stupid to take me off now."

"I'm really sorry, Joanne."

"You and me both. I'm really ticked off. Seems when I do something *I'm* proud of, I can't participate. But when I do something *he's* proud of, that's a different story. So I'm off curfew today. It's the old double standard!"

"Hold on, just slow down a minute." Cliff gave her one of his easygoing smiles. "I thought we were friends."

"We are."

"Well, then, shoot that thing in the other direction."

"What? Oh, my mouth."

"Good. Now calm down. I can understand why you're so upset about the play. But why don't you concentrate instead on what's happening today?"

"Cliff, this journalism thing isn't like the play. I just fell into it."

"You wrote the stories, didn't you?"

"Yes, but—"

He wagged a finger at her. "No 'yes-buts.' You either wrote them, or you didn't. They could have come from no one else. You're unique,

Joanne Palmer. When are you going to realize that?"

"You're wrong, Cliff. I'm a failure. Most of the time when I try to do something as myself, it's a total disaster!"

"What about the part in the play. That was you, you said. And you yourself earned the right to the competition today. Come on. Let's go see if your Color Day article wins."

She managed a smile as he nudged her. "OK. And Cliff—thanks."

"My pleasure." It was his turn for a bashful grin. He leaned over to shut her door.

Did he notice that electric shock she felt when this hand grazed her arm? Joanne wondered as they drove to the junior college. She stared at Cliff, startled. She'd never make it through the day as herself. Joanne Palmer was a nervous wreck.

There was only one lady who could carry her through with grace and style. *Hello, Barbra Streisand.*

Cliff didn't notice Barbra. Not at the registration. Not at the two seminars they attended on journalism as a career and journalism's changing role in society. Not even as they sat down to a free, if slight, luncheon of chicken à la king.

Or so Joanne thought.

He stared down at his plate for a long time after the chicken dish appeared.

"What is this stuff, anyhow?" Joanne chattered as she flicked a fork at it. "Well, eat up anyway. We only live once, whaddaya say?"

Cliff's steady gaze met hers. "Who are you doing, now?"

"What?" Joanne stopped, fork halfway to her mouth. "What do you mean?"

"You know what I mean. I haven't been sitting and talking to Joanne Palmer since we got out of the car. Am I that hard to be with?"

She dropped the fork. "Oh, no, Cliff. In fact . . ." She felt a flush starting. "Streisand," she blurted out. It was best to tell him the truth.

"Listen, she's a great lady to imitate—but do you really think she'd have gotten to where she is by imitating someone else?"

"Now *you* sound like someone else. My dad."

"Maybe once in a while you should listen," Cliff answered. Then he laughed at himself. "Lecture's over. Come on, Joanne, whoever you are. Spend the rest of the day with me."

Joanne looked up at Cliff and studied his clear, even-featured face. It hadn't been so tough being with him. As a matter of fact, it had been great. Joanne returned his smile and picked up her fork. She had a lot of thinking to do.

A few minutes later the head of the journalism department at the junior college moved to the microphone. Quickly a hush fell over the dining hall. Cliff took hold of Joanne's right hand and gave it a good-luck squeeze.

"Ladies and gentlemen. This time every year we meet to judge some of the reporters of the future. We're proud of them, and for them . . ."

Joanne listened in a daze, half-hearing the speech. She was shaken out of her near-trance by Cliff, who grabbed her arm when the man began to read the names of the winners.

"And in the feature article category, Miles Peterson, first place. Second place goes to Joanne Palmer. Third to Kerrie Grandling . . ."

Joanne's ears rang. "Me?" she whispered to Cliff, whose smile seemed to stretch across his entire face. She stood up.

"Yes, you!" Cliff cried, tightening his clasp on her arm.

"Let go of me," she said. "They're expecting me up there."

"Not until you decide who you are. And who won."

"Don't do this to me now."

He shook his head. "Somebody should have done this to you a long time ago."

People were staring at them. She twisted her arm slightly, but he held firm.

"Cliff!" she pleaded.

"There's no way you can mess this one up except by not being yourself."

"All right. All right." He let go. "I am me. Nobody else but me could get in a mess like this." She dashed out of his reach and up to the podium.

On the way home, she kept hugging her trophy. Cliff looked at her and grinned.

"You look like a kid with a full cookie jar," he said.

She laughed. "I never thought I'd say it, but this is great. This is really great!" She polished the metal plate on the front of the trophy.

"I do believe that's the real Joanne talking," Cliff said as he guided the car to a parking space on Joanne's street.

"You bet!" Joanne told him as he helped her out of the car. "Next time I'm tempted to do somebody else, I'll think of this."

"Good for you," Cliff said. They were at the front door, and he hesitated a second before asking, "I know you're on strict curfew and all, but do you think your dad would consider a study date or two?"

Joanne's heart soared. "I'll try," she said. "I don't know of anything I'd like more."

"I'll see you tomorrow then," Cliff said. "But in the meantime . . ." He bent over and gave her a kiss before walking back to his car.

Chapter Fourteen

The following day Joanne was working on her Spanish homework in study hall. Cliff was at the other side of the room, buried in a mass of paperwork of his own, but every now and then they would make eye contact and smile. Cliff didn't arouse the passions in her that Rob had. But what he did give her was something she was beginning to realize was far more valuable—a feeling of steadiness and reliability, a feeling that might turn into love, she thought.

About halfway through the period, the inter-office phone buzzed, and Mr. Bostwick seemed angry as he was forced to interrupt one of his jokes to answer it. As he hung up the phone, he called out, "Joanne Palmer. Is Joanne Palmer here?"

Puzzled, Joanne approached the teacher's desk. "Report down to the principal's office at once," he said.

Joanne went back to her desk to get her books. Cliff shot her a concerned glance. She shrugged, to indicate she was as confused as he was, and ran out of the room and down to Mr. Gatos's office.

The elderly secretary escorted Joanne to the large conference room adjacent to the principal's office. She gasped when she saw not only her mother but also her father sitting at the rectangular table. She didn't know what she'd done, but it had to have been something serious.

"Sit down over there, Joanne," Mr. Gatos said, pointing to an empty seat next to her mother. "We'll begin as soon as—" He looked up. "Oh, here she is now."

Joanne turned around and felt her heart nearly stop as Christina walked into the room, accompanied by Rob. Looking around the room, she saw that Ms. Kovelstein and Mr. Musselman were also there. No one was smiling.

"I'm afraid, Joanne," Mr. Gatos apologized, "we've had some serious allegations from Christina that affect not only your student status but also Mr. Musselman's career as a drama teacher here at Fremont." He cleared his throat. "We have to be sure it's not just a matter of sour grapes."

"I don't think that's called for," Rob interrupted. He backed off slightly as the principal shot him a look to be quiet.

Joanne gripped the arms of her chair. "What—what's happening?"

Mr. Gatos looked at her and her parents kindly. "First of all, Joanne, I want you to know this is not a kangaroo court. If I discover these allegations to be true, you and your parents will have to meet with the district superintendent. If we have to go that far, we're talking suspension."

"I don't have to tell you how that would affect your graduation, Joanne," Ms. Kovelstein said.

Joanne looked questioningly at her mother. Susan Palmer, looking drawn and tired, gave her daughter a tight-lipped nod. Her father stared straight ahead at the principal.

Rob, in the meantime, had taken a seat next to Christina and opposite Joanne. He looked like an ill-tempered statue.

"What did I do?" Joanne finally asked.

Christina took a *Trailblazer* out from under her arm and waved it in the air. "You and Mr. Musselman were playing games," she cried in a shrill voice. "I told Mr. Gatos the audition was rigged."

"Rigged?" said the Palmer family in one gasp.

"That's right," Christina shot back at Joanne. "You were so sure you'd get the part that

151

you didn't even want to read. It was Mr. Mussel-man who insisted that you read to make it look good."

"That's ridiculous," Joanne cried out. "I was there with Lynn Willis. She wanted to try out for Laurey. I never even thought of auditioning until I got there." Joanne appealed to her parents. "Mr. Musselman heard me helping Lynn while we were sitting in the audience. He insisted I try out if I had the nerve, so I did."

"That's correct," the drama teacher added angrily. "I heard her reading with a blond girl, Lynn. She sounded like she had potential, so I asked her to sing. She was perfect for Ado Annie. I chose Joanne because she had talent." He mopped his face with his white handkerchief. "Something this other young lady had very lit-tle of, I'm sorry to say. Those are the facts."

The significance of what was going on in the room came crashing down on Joanne, and she could hardly believe it. She knew Christina had been overly selfish, but never had she imag-ined she'd stoop to such meanness. But why was it so important to her? Joanne wondered.

Christina wouldn't have gone to so much trouble just for Rob. She had him—and if noth-ing else, Joanne's months of chasing him unsuc-cessfully should have shown her that.

Joanne also didn't believe Christina really wanted to play Ado Annie. She never struck Joanne as being the actress type—in their sophomore English class, Joanne remembered, Christina had refused to stand in front of the class and read Juliet to Brad Hennessey's Romeo.

That left only one reason for her behavior: pure spite. She would do anything she could to hurt Joanne—even jeopardize her graduation.

And what was Rob's part in all this? Joanne looked at him and couldn't believe she had wasted so much time pining over the loss of such a selfish person. He was so wrapped up in getting what he wanted that he didn't care whom he hurt. Whatever Christina wanted, Rob helped her to get.

But not this time, Joanne told herself. Remembering Mr. Musselman's words, she realized she really had earned that role—a role that, ironically, she had to give up anyway. But she was ready to fight for it. She wanted to fight to get the part back, fight the principal, *and* fight her parents. If nothing else, she wanted to prove that she, Joanne Palmer, could get passing grades, act in a play, date a boy, and still graduate with her class.

Mr. Gatos interrupted the momentary silence with an impatient wave of his slim, manicured hand. "I am waiting to hear anything significant, Christina. What specifically are you talking about, and where's the evidence you said you had?"

"Just this." Christina opened the *Trailblazer.*

Joanne recognized it as one of the first issues she had worked on.

"It's here in black and white." Christina spread the paper out triumphantly on the table. "In February the school put on a Greek play, *Antigone*." She badly mispronounced the name, saying "Auntie-gone." "Anyway, it bombed. But Mr. Musselman got together with Joanne. She wrote a good review and feature of it, just to serve his reputation. Obviously, her reward for that was the part in the senior play."

"I don't believe this," cried Joanne.

"That's right," Rob asserted. "It's in black and white."

"Joanne?" Ms. Kovelstein asked, looking worried.

Joanne twisted her hands in her lap, nervous but ready to defend herself. "Well, yes, I wrote a review. It wasn't meant to be either good or bad. I don't know Mr. Musselman, really. I'm not in any of his classes. I met him when I asked him if I could review the play. Lynn and I went to the *Antigone* dress rehearsal Tuesday after school. By the time the paper came out the following Monday, the show had already closed."

Mr. Musselman asked softly, "Did I at any time ask you to write a favorable review?"

"No."

"Did I promise you anything?"

"No."

"Would you have written anything I wanted you to write?"

Oh, don't ask me that, she thought. "No. That is, I don't think so," she said after a moment. "I—I have kind of a soft heart. And I honestly didn't think the play was so terrible. It was really heavy stuff, you know, and most of the kids didn't like it. I heard them talking after the paper came out, but I thought Mr. Musselman deserved a chance to say why he wanted to put it on in the first place."

Ms. Kovelstein took the paper away from Christina and sat back with it. She took a few seconds to skim the article. "I remember this. It's fairly unbiased."

Rob flexed his shoulders. "Look, this isn't getting us anywhere. Musselman isn't going to admit what he did, and neither is Joanne. But it's in print, and it's not the only time she's abused her position with the *Trailblazer*."

Everybody looked at him. He shrugged and casually said, "She tampered with the paper for me, too."

"Oh, Rob!" Joanne choked out. She looked at him, feeling a pain in her chest that made her breathing difficult. "What are you doing?" She knew she had lost everything. Rob was so anxious to have a winner that he was willing to possibly ruin his chances for a scholarship in the process.

He stuffed his hands in his pockets. "I had

155

a bad baseball game, the first away-game with Central High. I lost my temper and looked pretty bad. Joanne offered to pull the story about it if I'd take her to the Sadie Hawkins dance. We used to date, you see, and she really hates Christina for taking me away from her."

Mr. Gatos saw her stricken look. "Is this true, Joanne?"

She looked down at her lap. "Yes, but not the way he said it."

Her mother cried, "No, Joanne, honey!" The room was in an uproar.

Rob called over the din, "She admitted it. You heard her."

A cool, clear voice cut calmly through the noise. "I suggest we let Joanne finish her story. There is more here than meets the eye, if I know my daughter. And I think I do." Fred Palmer gave Joanne an encouraging nod. "Go on, honey."

Joanne folded her hands and tried to calm herself. "Rob was right," she repeated, all the while lacing and unlacing her fingers, unable to meet anyone's stare. "I thought I loved Rob." As her mother sucked in her breath, she added, "You know, in a high-school sort of way. I wanted to do anything to help him." She looked up and met Ms. Kovelstein's worried gaze. "The baseball game was a real disaster. Rob had a temper tantrum—several of them actually—on the field, and he almost got thrown out of the game. He wasn't going to practices, and it showed.

"Anyway, he came to me before the paper deadline and begged me to do something about the story. Not change the score or anything . . . but the paper goes to the state scouts, and Rob was in line for a state scholarship. I didn't know what to do."

She licked her lips. "I wanted to help him. I really care—I really cared for him. I figured a college scholarship was worth more than a story in a school paper. So I—ah—I threw the story away."

Christina gave a short, harsh laugh, tossing her blond mane back from her shoulders. Rob's gaze was fixed on her, but she couldn't read his expression. Joanne looked away from them.

"When the editor couldn't find the copy, they used someone else's version, one that didn't mention Rob's tantrum."

"What did you hope to accomplish by all this, Joanne?" her father asked softly. He alone did not seem disappointed in her.

"I hoped I'd save Rob's scholarship, of course. And—and I wanted him back. I couldn't see that he was just using me." Joanne took a long, shuddering breath. "He said he'd do anything to have the story changed, and I"—she dropped her eyes—"wanted to go to the dance so badly. So I made a deal, and Rob dumped me anyway. And now everyone knows."

"Did you ever think of going to Mrs. Stickney and asking her to handle the situation?" her counselor asked.

"Sure. At first I told Rob to go to her or to Simone, but he wouldn't do it. And he made me promise not to tell anyone else about it. But, honest, Ms. Kovelstein, I didn't do anything devious to get that part in the play. I earned that!"

The gray-haired principal shook his head. "I'm disturbed by the lack of good judgment here."

"Bad judgment is not a crime," Mr. Palmer pointed out.

"That's true," Ms. Kovelstein interjected.

Mr. Gatos added briskly, "So far all we have is a case of bad judgment. On Rob's part and on Joanne's—although it may have saved him a scholarship. I don't agree that it was handled properly, but it's over and done with." He sighed. "Mr. Musselman, the question returns to whether you and Joanne worked out an arrangement."

Mr. Musselman sighed and sat back in his chair. "I cannot disprove the accusation. Joanne was excellent, and as far as I'm concerned, she has the part."

Joanne looked at her mother and father and then, taking a deep breath, turned to face the drama teacher. "I don't think that's an issue, either. My parents have forbidden me to be in the play. I should have told you sooner, but I thought I could talk them into changing their minds, but they said no. So you went to all this for nothing, Christina. I can't even accept the part." To her horror, a single tear dropped down, and she brushed it away fiercely. She wouldn't cry in front of them. She wouldn't!

Mrs. Palmer added softly, "Mr. Gatos, do you think anyone would go through all this, just to turn around and give the part up?"

"No, Mrs. Palmer, I don't," answered the principal. He turned to Joanne and said, "I'm very sorry we had to put you through this. You, too, Mr. and Mrs. Palmer. I believe Joanne's innocent. And my deepest apologies to you, Mr. Musselman. As far as I'm concerned, the matter is closed."

"Thank you," Joanne said tearfully.

"As for you, Christina," Mr. Gatos said, turning his attention to the blond, "I'd like to have a few words with you, in private. Come see me in my office in five minutes."

"Yes, Mr. Gatos," Christina said contritely.

"You've got quite a girl there," Ms. Kovelstein said to Joanne's parents, who'd gathered around their daughter. "I'd reconsider her grounding, if I may say so. There will be no problem with her graduating."

Mr. Musselman paused in the doorway and

then turned and bowed courteously to the Palmers. "Good day. I, too, hope you reconsider your decision about the play. And you, young lady"—he glared at Christina—"if Joanne informs me she cannot accept the part, I want you to know you will not be considered under any circumstances." He followed Mr. Gatos and Ms. Kovelstein out of the door.

Chapter Fifteen

Suddenly only Christina and Rob were left. The tall blond jumped to her feet, wrapping her hands around Rob's arm. "I hate you, Joanne."

"Hate me if you have to," Joanne said tiredly. "I'm sorry. There are better things to do this spring than hate anybody."

Christina's lower lip trembled. Suddenly she sat down sobbing, her head bent over the table. "Oh, I can't stand it!" she cried. "Why do you do everything right?"

"Me? I've been grounded for the rest of the school year for my grades. You think that's fantastic?"

Christina sniffled. "When I first started going out with Rob, you were always there. If it wasn't at the baseball games, it was after lunch or after school. And then when all your articles started appearing in the *Trailblazer*, Rob was always talking about them and how funny you could be. Then when I try out for the senior play, there you are again." The sobs overcame her.

Joanne awkwardly stood on one foot and then the other. "I guess you just need to learn to be yourself, Christina," Joanne said. "I didn't set out to hurt you. Honestly."

Rob eyed Joanne. "I guess I owe you an apology," he said. "I should have known you couldn't do anything like that with Musselman. I have a bad temper, and I'm really sorry about it." He pulled Christina up by her arm and walked her to the door. "Good luck."

Christina raised her head, her eyes bleary. "I'm sorry, too, I guess. I—oh, well." She stumbled out the door with Rob.

Mr. Palmer, who'd been sitting with his wife in the opposite corner, got up and smiled at his daughter. "I'm proud of you, Joanne," he said.

She took a shuddering breath. "Of me? What about Barbara Walters or Doonesbury or any one of the other people I pretended to be? I told Christina to be herself. I should take some of my own medicine. All this stuff—it's not me."

"Oh, yes, it is," her father insisted. "I've watched you take the qualities of all those other people and slowly mold them into yourself. Most of us have an idol or two. It's just that you have many. There's nothing wrong with it, as long as you know where they end and the real Joanne begins."

The Palmers walked out of the conference room, and Joanne gasped when she saw Cliff waiting. "What are you doing here?" she cried.

"Thought you might need a little rescuing," he said, smiling. "Ms. Kovelstein just told me what happened. Everything fine now?"

"Couldn't be better," she said.

"I could think of one thing." Cliff cleared his throat. "Mr. Palmer, I hope you don't think badly of me for saying this, but I think Joanne deserves that part in the play."

Her father scratched his head and laughed. "You and the rest of the world, it seems. I guess I forgot what senior year was all about. Some of my best memories are of high school." He clasped Joanne's shoulder. "If you really think you can do it, Jo, then go for it."

"Thanks, Dad!" Joanne said, hugging him.

"I think we can ease up on your curfew, too," her mother added.

Mr. Palmer looked at Joanne and Cliff. "Well, I have to get back to the office. Coming, Susan?"

As soon as her parents left, Joanne hugged Cliff. "Thanks for being here," she said.

"I was concerned." Then, taking hold of her

hand he asked, "Would you like an escort back to class?"

"I couldn't think of anything I'd like better, Cliff."

Walking slowly down the hallway, Cliff asked, "How would you like to go to the senior class barbecue with me?"

She looked up at him. "Can you do Mick Jagger?"

He laughed. "No."

"Good. Do you do John Travolta?"

"No."

"How about Cliff Wright?"

"Naturally."

"Then I'd love to be your date." She squeezed his hand tightly.

He stopped then, took her books from her, and placed them on top of a nearby water fountain. Then he tilted her chin up and kissed her softly. She felt the warmth of his lean body and melted into his kiss. After a long, dizzying moment it ended. He moved away, holding onto her shoulders.

"Who was that I just kissed? Wow!"

"Me," she answered.

He smiled. "That's the best 'you' I've met yet." He pulled her close, and they kissed again.

Her heart fluttered as they broke apart. "I think I know what you mean. I promise you this Joanne Palmer will be around for a long, long time."

( ) **#30 LITTLE WHITE LIES** by Lois I. Fisher (**On Sale December 15, 1982 * #23102-2 * $1.95**)

Everyone says Nina has a good imagination—a gift for telling stories. In fact, it's one of her stories that attracts Scott to her. He's one of the Daltonites, the most sophisticated clique in the school. The Daltonites don't welcome outsiders, but Nina finds it so easy to impress them with a little exaggeration here, a white lie there. But her lies finally start to catch up with her, and Nina's afraid of losing Scott forever.

Buy these books at your local bookstore or use this handy coupon for ordering:

You'll fall in love with all the Sweet Dream romances. Reading these stories, you'll be reminded of yourself or of someone you know. There's Jennie, the *California Girl*, who becomes an outsider when her family moves to Texas. And Cindy, the *Little Sister*, who's afraid that Christine, the oldest in the family, will steal her new boyfriend. Don't miss any of the Sweet Dreams romances.

☐	22542	**LOVE SONG #19** Anne park	$1.95
☐	22682	**THE POPULARITY SUMMER #20** Rosemary Vernon	$1.95
☐	22607	**ALL'S FAIR IN LOVE #21** Jeanne Andrews	$1.95
☐	22683	**SECRET IDENTITY #22** Joanna Campbell	$1.95
☐	22840	**FALLING IN LOVE AGAIN #23** Barbara Conklin	$1.95
☐	22957	**THE TROUBLE WITH CHARLIE #24** Jaye Ellen	$1.95
☐	22543	**HER SECRET SELF #25** Rhondi Villot	$1.95
☐	22692	**IT MUST BE MAGIC #26** Marian Woodruff	$1.95
☐	22681	**TOO YOUNG FOR LOVE #27** Gailanne Maravel	$1.95
☐	23053	**TRUSTING HEARTS #28** Jocelyn Saal	$1.95
☐	23101	**NEVER LOVE A COWBOY #29** Jesse Dukore	$1.95
☐	23102	**LITTLE WHITE LIES** Lois I. Fisher	$1.95